C000112375

Colette

You Don't Have to Say You Love Me

Abigail Summer

Cover design: Deb Sutton

Copyright © Abigail Summer 2019

This book is a work of fiction

All names, characters, businesses, places, events, locales, and incidents are either the products of the author's imagination or used in a fictitious manner. Any resemblance to actual persons, living or dead, or actual events is purely coincidental.

Special thanks to:

My husband Alex, for his patience, support, and endless mugs of strong coffee.

My editor and friend Jackie, for her expert critique, advice, and encouragement.

My long-time friend Kay, for the countless hours on messenger beta reading and discussing the plot.

Tom Peashey, for giving feedback from an American reader's perspective.

Guernsey resident Luke, for reading the draft manuscript, and for his lovely comments.

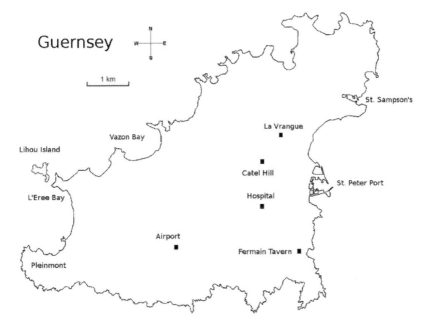

Guernsey

N
W   E
S

1 km

St. Sampson's

La Vrangue ■

Vazon Bay

Catel Hill ■

Lihou Island

L'Eree Bay

Hospital ■

St. Peter Port

Airport ■

Fermain Tavern ■

Pleinmont

Contents

Prologue

Thursday, June 13th 1968

A huge setting sun glinted on a steadily advancing tide. Gradually the stone causeway was being breached by lapping waves. A rare moment indeed, for this rocky Atlantic coast was more used to crashing surf. The tranquillity suited this warm June evening, perfect for a soul-searching moment alone.

I had to do it, didn't I? ... It's for the best, I know it is.

A reflected orange glow rose to meet a descending mirror image in the sky over Lihou Island. Colin waited for its spiritual aura to reach the Priory of St. Mary, bathing the ancient ruins in ethereal light. Soon Lihou would again be separated from Guernsey, the second largest of the British Channel Islands.

Can I handle it? ... I have to. I'm much stronger now.

Of all the fantastic places he'd discovered since coming to Guernsey, this headland to the north of L'Erée Bay was the most remote. And now the most meaningful too.

As Colette I was invincible ... wasn't I?

He recalled the first time Colette had come to this special place. Angry surf crashed on spray-smoothed boulders; they could hardly hear themselves speak. He remembered the laughter, the emotion, and the tears. But most of all he remembered the confusion; a perplexity of feelings that rose up from where they'd lain dormant for so many years. Emotions that even she, strong-willed and confident as she'd become, had succumbed to. How deeply affected

1

she'd been by events that were destined to change her life forever.

Giving up isn't easy. In fact, it hurts like hell.

The cooling air stroked Colin's long blond hair. Wearily he brushed a wisp from his tired, blue eyes.

The bottom line is, a baby needs its father.

Tomorrow he would leave this enchanting isle. Someday, when the hurt had subsided, he would return. Maybe not for a long time, and almost certainly as a very different person, but his eyes would absorb this breath-taking view again one day.

"Think of the future," she said ... What future is there for someone like me?

Now so low that Lihou Island was leached of all detail, the setting sun created a silhouette, backlit by a brilliant corona that flared once, held for a few seconds, then began the inevitable transition from day to night. A movement behind him, her hand on his shoulder, he looked up. Leanne's face, tinged red from the fading sunset reminded him of happier times, but a tear on her cheek showed she too was hurting.

Her secret smile. I fell for it, but she knew.

Colin hugged himself in the approaching dark. A chill shiver set his mind wandering into the past.

Would I do it all over again? ... I'd have no choice.

Chapter 1 – Dear Mr Cameron

Ipswich - Sunday, January 15th 1967

"Sam's on the phone for you, Colin," his mother called up the steep, narrow stairs. "Keep it short, your father's waiting for a call from work."

He put down his handwritten song sheet and leaned his battered acoustic guitar against a chair beside his bed. "Be right down."

Even though she now lived in Devon, his old school friend, Samantha, cared enough to stay in touch. "There's an advert in the Exeter Star for a young, experienced boatbuilder, Colin."

"I'm happy where I am, Sam. And anyway, I'm on the east coast. Bloody miles away!"

"It doesn't matter! The job's at a new boatyard in the Channel Islands, Guernsey to be precise, and there's accommodation provided. With nearly five years' experience, you'd walk it!"

He fidgeted with a directory on a shelf under the wall telephone. "I like the people I work with. God knows, I don't have many other friends."

"Come on, Colin. Spread your wings. Think of all that sunshine and groovy girls. Just kidding about the girls, sorry!"

Colin grinned. He was used to Sam's teasing. "I'll leave the sexy chicks to you, Sam. By the way, how is the gorgeous Trina?"

"She's cool. As usual, she can't get enough, but that's too much information. She's taking her finals next month, then she'll be a fully-fledged staff nurse. Listen to me. You simply must apply for this job. I know you too well. You'll never get to where you ought to be by holding on to apron strings, however comforting that might be."

"Sounds like I have no choice."

"You don't."

He gave a defeated sigh. "Go on then, give me the details. I'll think about it."

Back in his room, Colin repeated over and over an improvised countermelody for *You Don't Have to Say You Love Me*. His unbroken vocal range perfectly emulated Dusty Springfield's. But since Sam's phone call he couldn't concentrate, and the sadness of the song made him wonder whether his life was on the right track. He put down his guitar and looked again at the slip of paper with the Guernsey address. Picking up his songwriting notepad, he scribbled a first line: Dear Mr Cameron...

*

The black cab ride from Liverpool Street Station to the West End filled Colin with awe; the Bank of England, St. Paul's Cathedral, and Smithfield Market. But when he paid the driver and turned to the grand entrance of the Strand Palace Hotel, he suddenly felt quite small and wished he was back home in Ipswich.

"It's good of you to travel to London, Colin. We like to keep things informal, so please call me James, and this is my wife, Leanne. Your letter said you have several years' experience fitting out pleasure cruisers, and that's just the sort of talent we need."

As interviews go, he thought, this one was a doddle. As Sam had predicted, he'd 'walked it.' A bit odd though, that sultry gaze from Leanne when he accepted the job offer, as though she was saying, *'Shh ... don't tell anyone, this is just between us.'*

The two-hour train ride from Ipswich meant he'd left home at six-thirty. He'd eaten the sandwiches his mother had made him hours ago, so a lunch invitation was more than acceptable. And Leanne's secret smile intrigued him.

"Nothing like a first-class meal with good company." James tore off a chunk of naan bread and scooped up chicken biryani. "I expect you'd like to know a bit about us, wouldn't you?"

Colin nodded, pointed to his mouthful of food, and shrugged one shoulder. Both shoulders might have signalled disinterest. He glanced at Leanne. He was actually very interested indeed.

"Can't you see he's eating, James?" Leanne brushed a curl from her cheek. "Us blondes have to stick together, don't we, Colin?"

Gulping down a spoonful of spicy daal gosht, he made an awkward face. "I was thinking of having my hair cut short, fresh start new image…"

"Don't you dare! It's gorgeous as it is. Long hair is becoming super cool, too."

James glared at Leanne. "Save your compliments for when he arrives in Guernsey."

She touched Colin's hand. "Don't mind my husband, he's a stuffy old businessman. We'll start our own mutual appreciation society,

5

eh?"

James quelled her with another glare. "We have two children, although my wife seems to forget that sometimes. I'm semi-retired from my advertising agency that has grown to be the largest in Scotland. As the board chairman, I'll be staying at my parents' house near Kinross from time to time."

"James got bored with retirement, Colin. After all, there's only so much golf a man can play. The boatyard at St. Sampson's is our latest venture. That's why we need someone skilled like you."

"Quite so, Leanne. Colin, I think you'll be comfortable in the apartment we've recently renovated. It's above our large detached garage. The balcony overlooks Leanne's kitchen and, heaven forbid, you could even wave to each other if you have a mind to."

"Don't be so stodgy, James. Your pad is lovely, Colin. Victorian features and everything, a wood burning stove too. There's a second bedroom for family or friends who want to stay over, and we've put in a modern bathroom and kitchen, but left the decoration for you to do. There's nothing worse than living with someone else's colour scheme."

On the train home, Colin closed his eyes and pictured what life on Guernsey would be like. But things rarely turned out the same as he envisaged. His vivid imagination and Bohemian outlook often conjured quite a different reality. St. Sampson's was the second largest port in Guernsey, according to Leanne. He decided he'd pay a visit to the public library; they were sure to have books on the

Channel Islands.

Two weeks later, a letter postmarked Guernsey, Tuesday, February 14th arrived. He wasn't superstitious, but was inclined to think that a travel document posted on his nineteenth birthday was a good omen for a safe journey. He'd never seen an airline ticket before. In fact, he'd never been further off the ground than the viewing platform at the top of the Post Office tower in London. So nothing could surpass the delight of holding this Channel Airways cheque-sized booklet with his name typewritten in capital letters on both inside pages. At last, he was on his way.

Leaving parties with colleagues and with family at home. Reading up on the history, culture, and economy of Guernsey, and visiting a cousin who'd been there. Writing to Samantha and Trina with the good news. Mother's tears and Father's advice. The last four weeks had been hectic. But now, standing in the bay window of his parents' terraced house, impatiently waiting for a taxi to arrive, his new life was about to begin.

*

Colin took his holdall down from the rack, slung it over his shoulder, shuffled along the aisle, then thirteen steps down onto the tarmac—he'd counted them. Scanning the expectant faces behind the safety fence next to the tiny arrivals hall, he was glad to see Leanne's blonde curls and secret smile.

"Hey, you made it! Good flight?"

"Relieved to be here, Leanne. I've never flown before."

"Is your whole life in that holdall, or do you have luggage?"

"Just my toolbox. It should have been transferred at Southend."

Leanne looked worried. "I brought my Mini Cooper. Will it fit do you think?"

"Yeah, only hand tools. It'll sit on the boot lid, and I'll secure it with a bungee."

For the first mile or so, along pretty country roads to the Camerons' home in La Vrangue, he found himself studying Leanne's appearance in more detail than at their first meeting in London. His eye for colour and form appreciated how her makeup matched her mini-dress, how its design revealed her shapely thighs and generous cleavage.

"You're quiet, Colin! I don't bite, you know. Well, not in a nasty way."

"Sorry, I'm a bit uptight. All this is new to me, and I don't know what you like to talk about."

"Oh, I'll chat about anything pretty much. How about I tell you about me, eh? That'd be a start wouldn't it?"

Leanne's friendly tone made him smile. "Yeah, I guess it would."

"Right, I'm married to James, but you already knew that. I have two children, seven-year-old boy and girl twins. I'll introduce you later. I love pop music, especially The Beatles and Donovan. James is forty-five, and I'm fifteen years younger. You can work that out for yourself…"

"Really? I thought you were younger than thirty."

"Nice one, Colin. Just the thing a girl needs to hear at my age! I moved to Guernsey with James five years ago when he semi-retired. I'm into modern fashions like Patti Boyd and Mary Quant. Being trendy is fab. And I simply adore blond young men who sit next to me in my car studying my dress and makeup. How's that? Oh, and I'm a good listener, too."

"You were kidding about blond young men, weren't you?"

She gave a sly look. "I'll keep you guessing on that. Your turn, Colin."

"I'm boring really. You don't wa..."

"No, you're not! It's only people who can't be bothered to listen who think you're boring. You fascinate me, so go on."

"Well, I live with mum and dad, or I did until this morning. I'm a good boatbuilder, or so everyone says. I don't have many friends, but that doesn't bother me…"

"Not even a girlfriend?"

"Not in the way you mean, Leanne, no. I play the guitar, but couldn't bring it on the plane with me. I write songs and poetry as a hobby, and I've been to art school."

Leanne grinned. "That's why you were studying my makeup was it? Colour harmony and all that."

"I couldn't figure out how your lipstick, whatever it's called, goes with your blue eyeshadow and dress. But it does."

"It's called Marshmallow Pink. Just let me know when you want to try it yourself," Leanne quipped, as she drove through tall open wrought iron gates and along a tree-lined gravel driveway. "Although I think a slightly darker shade would suit you better. Poor you, you're embarrassed now, I'm sorry. Don't mind me, I think we'll get along just great."

Chapter 2 - An extraordinary moment

A few yards across a flagstone courtyard at the side of the Camerons' granite-built manor house, Colin's apartment was far better than anything he could have imagined. Over a glass or two of wine one evening, Leanne explained that it originally housed a coachman and other outdoor servants. The old brick-built stables and carriage-house underneath were now a well-equipped garage for her red Mini and James' white Jaguar.

Although basic furnishings were provided, he soon made his new home comfortable with other items surplus to the Camerons' requirements. One gem of a find was an old bakelite radio that only crackled and hissed, until he strung a wire antenna from the living room window to a tall elm tree a few yards away. He'd never cooked for himself before, but quickly became adept at producing dishes which didn't look exactly like the glossy photographs in the recipe books Leanne had given him, but tasted delicious, especially when eaten at a glass-topped bamboo table out on the balcony.

*

After a couple of days settling into his apartment, Colin rode with James in his Jaguar to start work.

"Sorry, Colin. I can't hang about, I'm already late for an appointment in St. Peter Port. The two men I've already set on will get you up to speed. Bob and Frank are doing preparatory work at the moment. The fibreglass hulls are due next week, then all hell will be let loose."

Hefting his toolbox through large grey double doors, open flush to a corrugated façade, Colin took in his surroundings. The lofty, steel-roofed building, was spacious enough to accommodate two thirty-five-foot cruisers in parallel. A ventilated area with woodworking machinery was situated on one side, on the other, an office and reception area, with long horizontal windows, overlooking where the boats would be constructed. At the far end, a breeze wafted in through another set of big double doors, revealing a sizeable yard area with storage sheds beyond.

Being the new boy, he was uneasy, but his nervousness soon disappeared when the two older men welcomed him with a freshly brewed mug of coffee and a friendly chat in the welfare room next to the office. A couple of weeks before, they'd left their jobs at a long-established but declining boatyard just along a track towards the main road.

As the first few days passed, a team was established. Each knew what their responsibilities would be, aware also that overlap and flexibility were top priority, as is the way in small boatyards.

Being just as skilled at wielding an adze as he was at fashioning a perfectly fitting pantry door, Colin assisted with the fabrication of substantial wooden frames with strong upright stanchions. The work was rough and heavy, but the timber supports were necessary to accommodate the cruisers, from the day they arrived as bare fibreglass hulls, until the completed craft were transported to a public slipway less than a quarter of a mile away.

Colin enjoyed decorating, and with Leanne's help, after the twins were in bed, it was fun too. They laughed together and gossiped about everyone and everything. They hugged when one of them was sad; he feigned embarrassment when she flirted with him; they sang along to their favourite songs on the pirate pop station, Radio Caroline, that they both became addicted to.

"Just look at you, Colin!"

"Eh? That doesn't make sense."

"The mirror! Go and look at your hair. You've got white paint all over the back."

"How am I supposed to see the back of my hair in a mirror, Leanne?"

"Idiot! Get yourself into that bathroom and I'll wash it for you. Emulsion's a pig to get off once it's dry!"

"Bloody hell, I can hardly breathe," he spluttered, as she rinsed his hair for the third time.

"Just stay where you are over the basin. I'll fetch a towel."

"Make it quick will you, my sodding eyes are stinging!"

"Oh, poor old you. Now you know what us girls have to go through at the hairdresser."

Carefully drawing strands of Colin's hair through the towel, Leanne kissed his cheek and spoke softly. "I never had a sister, but if I did, I'd want her to be just like you, sweetheart."

*

By the middle of August, the first cruiser was nearing completion. She was to be called *St. Terethe*; a clever anagram thought up by her buyer who was a leading actor in a popular English soap opera, affectionately referred to as The Street. Colin met more of the cast when the owner brought them to see his boat in mid-construction, and he felt proud when one famous actress admired his skilful joinery.

The second boat, as yet unsold, was assembled. Her bulkheads, stern tubes, and engines were installed, but she now lay idle while everyone worked on *St. Terethe* to meet the agreed launch date in September.

*

Colin stretched out on his comfy sofa, flipping through the pages of his thesaurus. He was searching for a word that would rhyme with Lovers to end the last line of a song he was writing. Mothers, Brothers, and Others were not appropriate, and Covers, Smothers, and Suffers didn't fit the theme. He was about to give up in despair when familiar footsteps on the outside stairway gave him fresh hope. While Leanne took his place on the sofa, he uncorked a bottle.

"What are you on about, Colin? Lovers is a perfectly good word to use."

"But I can't find a word or phrase to rhyme with it."

"Then use your imagination! It doesn't have to make sense. No-one understands song lyrics these days anyway ... take *Whiter Shade of Pale* for instance."

"You're right. I need to come up with something weird, don't I?"

"That shouldn't be too difficult! Now please put that bloody notepad away. I need your attention. Something important has come up, and it will affect you."

He poured their wine and seated himself in an armchair opposite Leanne. It was unlike her to be this serious during an evening visit.

"James will tell the lads at the yard tomorrow, but because you're now almost part of the family he wants me to outline the situation to you tonight. We were planning for me to start work in the office so that he could help with the boats..."

"We could do with an extra pair of hands on the shop floor that's for sure, Leanne."

"Well, we've employed a young local woman for the twins. She seems capable enough, and the kids like her, but she's a bit too well-proportioned for a nanny if you ask me. James is satisfied with her though, and I don't mean just her friendly smile!"

"What did you mean by *were?* Are you saying you won't be coming to work at the yard?"

"Be patient, I'll get to that shortly. This isn't easy for me you know." She took several sips of her wine. "The house is due for renovation, but you already knew that."

"Gradually, over the next three years isn't it?"

"Not anymore! James' golfing friend who owns the building company has financial problems. Some imbecile at the planning department has refused the demolition of a dilapidated old tomato

15

vinery, on land he bought to build houses on."

"That's a pain, but how does that affect you?"

"You know James, like a knight in shining armour he's riding to the rescue."

"Surely, shouldn't 'Sir Jamesalot' be saving damsels in distress, not rescuing builders?"

"You're probably right, Colin, and no way could you describe Derry Norman as a damsel. He's six feet four and built like a brick shithouse. Anyway, to keep him solvent, the work on the main house has been brought forward. From next week you'll be overlooking a sodding building site."

"Won't bother me, but what are you and James going to do?"

"You mean what am I going to do. James is buggering off to Scotland before the weekend. There's trouble at the agency that he has to sort out."

"Nothing too serious I hope ... is it?"

"No, not serious, Colin. It's bloody catastrophic, that's what. That arsehole of a general manager James hired last year has only gone and started a rival company, and taken some staff and big-bucks clients with him. You can't trust anyone these days."

"The bastard! You won't be coming to work at the yard then. You'll have to be here for the children if James is away, won't you?"

"With the house being a mess for a long time, we've decided that the twins will be better off with their grandparents where James will be staying. There's an excellent local private school they can attend when the new term starts in September."

Colin stared at the ceiling. It seemed like his whole world was falling apart.

"Hey, sweetheart. It'll be alright, I promise. But I will need your help."

"Anything, Leanne. Just say."

"Well, unlike you, I know zilch about building boats. In fact, I don't know much about anything mechanical. So, don't laugh when I tell you that 'yours truly' will be running the yard while James is away. There's no alternative."

"I'm not laughing, Leanne. *St. Terethe* is due for launching in four weeks' time!"

"And don't I know it. But you could manage the practical side of things, couldn't you? And I could concentrate on the commercial side. What do you say?"

He studied his wine glass. This proposition needed some thought; he'd never been in a position of responsibility before. "Uh, well … we would make a good team, I guess."

"We would, but you'll have to be promoted to foreman. James insists."

"I'm only nineteen, and…"

"You can do it, I know you can! I won't be able to manage without you. Please don't say no."

He grimaced defeat. "You know damned well I'd never let you down, Leanne. When do I start?"

"On Monday … James is leaving for Scotland with the children and their new nanny in two days' time. They're booked on the eleven-thirty flight to Southampton on Friday morning, then by hire car to Kinross. But listen, I've got to be nice to you because there's something else I need."

"Oh really! How much?"

Raising a wry eyebrow at his misguided humour, Leanne hesitated. "It'll be uncomfortable in the main house with all the dust and sweaty builders running about. Mmm, now there's a tempting thought." She gave a cheeky grin. "And it'll be lonely, too. Can I have your spare bedroom? Please, pretty please?"

He couldn't speak for the sudden lump in his throat, but his delighted expression said it all. Leanne sharing the apartment was something he'd imagined but never thought would happen.

Kneeling in front of him, Leanne took his hands and held them to her cheek. "Thank you," she whispered. "I'd have cried for a month if you'd said no."

They giggled like immature schoolgirls. While Leanne switched on a dim table lamp and turned the radio on low, he topped up their glasses. And when she seated herself on the carpet with her back to him, he knew it was her sign that she needed pampering.

"Bloody hell, Colin, who've you been practising on? Your neck massage is usually good, but tonight it's delicious!"

"I'll put a card in the newsagent's window, shall I? Masseuse for hire, Leanne Cameron recommended."

"Silly sod … Oh, wow! You've hit the spot just there. Yes, a little harder, that's it. What are you doing to me, Colette? That is so bloody sexy."

"Colette?"

"You said 'masseuse.'"

Colin grinned at his mistake. "Um, so I did."

Whether it was the wine or just another of Leanne's spontaneous embarrassment games, he wasn't at all surprised when she stood up, kicked off her sandals, and slipped the thin straps of her dress off her shoulders. And when it fell silently to the floor, it was also no surprise to see she was wearing nothing but her secret smile; this was Leanne after all.

She often did stupid things to shock him, and he'd got used to that. But this time it looked like she had something more intimate in mind. A sexual encounter with Leanne wasn't something he'd considered. In fact, it wasn't something he needed with anyone. But he knew he must react in some way, or this extraordinary moment would be lost forever.

The piano introduction of a Moody Blues song came to his rescue. Whispering the words of *Go Now*, he approached Leanne and brushed a strand of hair from her cheek.

Their eyes locked, a shared but futile search for a reason, any reason, to break away, both knowing that a wrong word or move would destroy the magic.

Leanne's fingers unbuttoning his shirt deepened his breaths; a light scratch of her fingernails triggered an unwelcome arousal. He pulled her close, her breast heaving against his chest, her lips warm and moist.

With another secret smile, she took his hand and led him into his bedroom.

Chapter 3 – Why me?

Colin was still fast asleep when Leanne crept out of the apartment, tiptoeing down the outside stairway to cross the courtyard.

Undressing in her own bedroom, she slipped into bed as softly as she could. But a drowsy grunt from her husband told her he was awake. "Sorry James, did I disturb you?"

"Uh, yeah, what time is it?"

"Judging by the dawn chorus, I'd say half five or so. You want me to check?"

"No, don't bother. Everything alright?"

"He's sleeping like a baby, I'll tell you later."

"All going to plan then." James smiled to himself and lifted an arm for her to snuggle into.

*

On Saturday morning, Colin spotted Leanne leaving the main house. He waved and was elated when she blew him a kiss in return. She hadn't been avoiding him after all.

"Sorry I haven't seen you since Wednesday," she shouted, "be back around half four. Is there anything you need?"

"Don't think so. It'll be hot in town today, take care."

"There's a hat in the car, and you worry too much, but thanks."

Continuing with his Saturday chores, he made sure everything was in its proper place. Leanne was moving in today, and he knew she was fussy about tidiness.

Despite forcing himself to think about other things, his mind kept returning to how attractive Leanne's hair had looked tied up with side curls framing her shades. It reminded him of a ribbon she'd left in the apartment some time ago. He'd meant to return it, but it was comforting to have it draped over a family photograph on his dressing table.

Sitting in front of the mirror, he brushed his hair up high and tied the pink satiny fabric in a neat bow. He put on sunglasses, releasing strands of hair to fall at either side. His reflection stared dolefully back at him.

Why me? ... Life is so unfair.

Late in the afternoon, the sound of Leanne driving into the garage disturbed a well-earned nap. He made it to the balcony just in time to see her emerge from under the apartment carrying several store bags.

She turned to see if he was there. "Won't be long, about twenty minutes I should think. I'll bring a few things over with me. The rest you can help me with tomorrow. Is that all right?"

"Yes sure," he said, pointing to the shopping bags. "Looks like you've been busy on the High Street."

"Guernsey's champion bargain hunter, that's me!" Turning towards the house, she hesitated. "By the way, Colin. Love the ribbon, it suits you."

"Ah ... it's fab, isn't it? I'm starting a new trend. All the lads will be wearing their hair like this one day."

"Yeah, right. A follow-on from Flower Power I suppose." Smiling mischievously to herself, Leanne disappeared into the house.

Colin fingered the pink ribbon in his hair. He wasn't embarrassed about it, but if he removed it, she might think he was ashamed and probably wouldn't mention it again. If he left his hair tied up, she'd likely make a joke about it. This he didn't mind. The ribbon would stay put, at least until she arrived.

Just before five, he heard footsteps on the stairway, the rustling of store bags, and the squeak of Leanne's bedroom door opening. He made a mental note to oil the hinges.

"You've worked hard, Colin, thank you," she shouted, then came into the kitchen where he was stirring a Dutch Oven simmering on the hob. "That smells delicious. I'm famished!"

"It's been three days, Leanne. Three bloody days. I've been going nuts!"

Stroking back his hair, she kissed his cheek. "Hey, we'll talk this evening, yeah? And if you're good, I might have a surprise for you. How long before we eat do you think? I need a soak."

He glanced at a timer he'd set for an hour. "Thirty minutes or so yet, you'll be fine."

The sound of Leanne splashing around in the bathroom made him smile. The apartment always seemed more like a home when she was here.

"There's something I need to know," she shouted. "It's about your rules."

Now he was intrigued. Creeping along the narrow hallway, he

paused by the open bathroom door.

"Come in, silly."

He perched on the edge of the lime green and gold wicker chair he'd painted to match the interior.

"Colin," she started, in a pseudo-official tone. "I have to know your apartment rules on nudity and keeping the bathroom door open."

"Stupid sod!" He made an indignant funny face. "Did you call me away from the kitchen just to ask a daft question?"

She gave him an impish look. "Luv the ribbon … Colette."

With Leanne's muffled bathroom song behind him, and her words flashing in his mind like a neon sign, he returned to the kitchen. She'd called him 'Colette' again. His thoughts wandered to other things she'd said. The remark about lipstick the day she picked him up from the airport, and the time she'd implied he was like a sister.

Leanne appeared at the kitchen door wearing a pink bathrobe, her hair in a white towel turban.

He slid freshly perked coffee along the countertop. "We're eating indoors, so put on something cool. You've got ten minutes."

She held the mug with both hands, inhaling the aroma of her favourite Columbian. "Jeans and a blouse? Or that little blue dress you like?"

"Oh, I don't know … wear the dress. Now bugger off while I set the table."

Dressed and back in the kitchen, Leanne rinsed her faded Fab

Four coffee mug and placed it upturned on the draining board. Mild expletives came from the living room and she glanced at the serving hatch. "Can't be that bad, Colin, what's up?"

"I'm folding the serviettes into boat shapes."

"That's nice, but why the swearing?"

"Pissing things have turned out like pirate hats!"

"Oh really? Well, shiver me timbers Jim lad. I'll have you walk the plank for that, you scurvy sea dog!"

When he placed the salad bowl and a plate of homemade corn tortillas on the dining table, Leanne was grinning at little Jolly Roger flags on cocktail sticks embellishing the serviettes. "What else could I do?" he said.

"You do make me laugh, Colin, and I love you for it. Pink ribbon and all!"

Fetching an earthenware dish from the kitchen, he placed it on an ornate cast iron trivet in the centre of the table. "Your favourite Pico de Gallo, Leanne. Welcome to your new home."

Pulling him close, she kissed his cheek. "You sure know how to treat a girl. Thank you." Lining a wrap with lettuce, she spooned filling on top. "This is a treat, not having to cook. You should apply for an evening job at the Steak & Stilton."

He knew the restaurant well. He'd been there several times with Leanne and James. The window tables had the most fantastic view over St. Peter Port, taking in the inner harbour in the foreground with its permanent moorings, and in the distance, the outer harbour entrance with the ferry terminal to the left and Castle Cornet to the right.

He scooped salad onto a tortilla. "I don't think I'd look good in one of those funny chef's hats."

"No silly, as a waitress!"

"What, and have your old man slap my arse like he did to that poor girl last time we were there?"

"You know she enjoyed it. Or if she didn't, the generous tip James gave her would have made up for it."

Colin thought about James and the twins' journey to Kinross. "Any news from Scotland yet?"

"James called this morning before I went out. They arrived at his parents' house in the early hours. The journey wasn't great though. Both kids threw up in the car, one of them over the nanny. Serves her right! Why should she be having a high old time with my husband while I'm stuck here running a sodding boatyard?"

"Aw, come on Leanne, you know you don't mean that."

"I do too!" she said, pulling a face at him.

"How'd it go in town today? Emptied the shelves in Creasey's did you?" he asked.

"You know me too well. As usual, I bought heaps of clothes and shoes I'll probably never wear. I'll show you later."

Colin wasn't listening. A small, peculiar-looking bug had abandoned its recent perch on the cruet handle and was taking pea-sized bites from the edge of a crisp lettuce leaf by the salad bowl. He leant close to study it. "Um, your husband mentioned something about having the telephone moved," he said, trying to decide what the insect was and what he should do with it.

"They're coming next Wednesday morning. Moving the existing line over here and putting a new one in for us to use. We can have extensions in our bedrooms if you like. They might be bugged though."

"Eh?"

"Bugged, get it? … If you were paying attention, you'd see I was pointing at your creepy-crawly friend."

"Idiot!"

He picked up the lettuce leaf complete with the strange-looking insect, wrapped it in his serviette, and shook it out over the balcony rail. Returning to the table, he poured another glass of white wine; neither he nor Leanne were keen on red.

After washing the dishes, they took chilled Chardonnay out onto the balcony, where a gentle breeze provided some respite from the humid atmosphere indoors. As the last rays of evening sunshine faded, gradually giving way to the approaching shadow of the elm tree, a song thrush created a welcome calmness. They both settled back with a sigh, enjoying the peaceful close to a hot and hectic day.

Leanne broke the silence. "It's time to talk, sweetheart. I'll go first then it's your turn, yeah?"

"That's fair I guess, go on." He hoped she was about to answer all the questions that had spun around in his head for the past three days.

"To understand me better, you need to know how it is with James and me. It might seem odd to you, but our marriage is quite unconventional. Some years ago, we decided that, although our sex life was great, we both needed a certain amount of variety. The problem for me, though, is that the variety always seems to be in James' favour. Did you know he's had lots of affairs?"

Feeling more than out of his depth, Colin thought it best to keep quiet.

"I'll take that as a no then. Of course, I knew about them all, poor bitches. But when James became bored with retirement, and we bought the boatyard, I hoped he'd employ someone who I'd, well, get along with, if you know what I mean, and he was cool with that. I liked you instantly when you came to London. I did try to let you know. Did you notice?"

"The secret smile … and like a fool I fell for it!"

"Oh, Colin, don't. It's not like that."

"Like what then? Like you'd rather I jumped into bed with you whenever you snap your fingers?"

"Please don't be angry. I am so very glad it was you."

"Don't patronise me, Leanne. You're only making it worse. I'm confused enough as it is."

"You're confused? I'm confused, too! You think I'm a selfish whore, and you'd be right, but my egocentric plan backfired on me, didn't it!"

28

"Oh, now I get it, I'm not man enough for you. Is that what you're saying?"

"Yes, that's exactly what I'm saying. You're not man enough for me, because since I met you, I've realised it's not a man that I need. Instead of a part-time lover, I've found a soul mate. Someone special I can share laughter and sadness with. Someone who fills my thoughts when they're not around. An extraordinary person who I'm so happy to have in my life. In short, Colin, I've found you!"

"Now I feel terrible, I thought you..."

"Don't even say it. I know what I am. But with you it's different, because you're different. You want the truth, even if it hurts?"

Expecting the inevitable, he nodded and braced himself.

"I think you've been suppressing your true feelings for a long time. Call it what you will, intuition if you like..."

"Intuition or perception?"

"Both! So here goes. I believe there's a sensuous female locked away inside you, just screaming to be released ... now tell me I'm wrong."

A kind of fear rose in his stomach. Once a secret is shared, it no longer exists, and he'd become accustomed to his secret, even though it tormented him constantly.

"I can't tell you you're wrong, Leanne ... and you know it."

Unaware of his inner turmoil, she continued. "But sometimes my feelings towards your female side scare me, and that's something I'm having trouble coming to terms with. When I shared your bed the other night, you probably thought I wanted sex, but I didn't. I just wanted to show you that I care ... and to be as close to 'Colette' as I could."

Colette!

He stared at his wine glass. When that dissolved into watery ripples, he held his breath and blinked puddles at the elm tree. There was no escape. At last, as if admitting to a crime he'd been born with, he faced his accuser. The relief was overwhelming.

A single tear trickled down his cheek, then another, and another, until he was sobbing uncontrollably.

Leanne held him close, his tears seeping through the thin cotton of her dress. "Let it go, sweetheart, it's all right. I'm here for you."

His sobs subsided and he muttered an apology.

"Shh," she soothed, "hey, mates yeah?"

He pressed his face to her bosom. The softness of her breast, her womanly aroma. He felt safer than he had for a long time.

The shadow of the elm tree now slanted across the balcony. It was time to go inside.

Leanne ran a bath for him, and while he reclined in the scented foam, she sat in the wicker chair. "As I said before, Colin, I'm a good listener."

He took a deep breath. Where to begin? "When I was young, before I went to school I mean, I was confused. Adults don't bother to explain why the kids they dress in shorts are called boys, and the ones they dress in frocks are called girls. Young as I was, I couldn't figure out why I was dressed in shorts and called a boy. Sometimes, though, I thought it was all just part of growing up, that one day it would be my turn and, at last, I'd be the little girl who had lots of friends, not the little boy who had lots of girlfriends … but it never happened."

"Are you alright, Colin? You don't have to do this you know."

"It's important for me, Leanne. I'm nineteen, and I've never been able to tell anyone before."

"I've never thought how a simple label, like boy or girl, can affect a child at such a young age. Growing up must have been difficult for you, sweetheart."

"It wasn't 'difficult' Leanne. For me, it was a bloody nightmare. School was shit! I knew I wasn't like the other boys, and they knew it too. I tried getting tough, but they still beat up on me. One on one wouldn't have been so bad, but you can't do much when there's a gang of them."

Leanne shook her head. "Children can be so cruel."

"Sam was my friend, though. Her name was Samantha, but she hated that. Sam was scary. The bullies left me alone when she was around. We were great pals, a bit like Tarzan and Jane, but in reverse. We still keep in touch. She was the one who told me about your vacancy and insisted I apply. Her girlfriend, Trina, had seen the ad in their local paper."

Leanne looked thoughtful. "If Trina hadn't seen that advert, I'd never have met you. It's spooky how such a small thing can bring

31

"people together and change their lives. Sorry, I am listening, go on."

"I really struggled with the lessons at school, never could figure out how most of the stuff would be any use after I left. I mean, I'll never be an Einstein or write a bestselling novel, so what good is 'order of operations' or 'past participles' to someone like me?"

"Buggered if I know. Maths and English always bored me to tears."

"I preferred practical things. The woodworking classes were great. When I left school soon after my fifteenth birthday, I got a job at a boatyard. It was brilliant working with real craftsmen. I grabbed all the overtime I could get, not just because I needed the money, but because the only real friends I had were at work."

"What about your weekends and evenings?"

"Yeah, it's not easy sitting in your room staring at the walls. After starting work, I enrolled at art school on Saturday mornings, got pretty good at it too. It taught me to appreciate colours and patterns, like the way mahogany and bird's-eye maple go really well together."

"Like my lipstick when I picked you up from the airport, eh?"

"You must have thought I was some sort of weirdo!"

"You know I love freaky people, Colin."

"That just about sums me up, I guess. Anyway, one of the students used to arrive with a guitar slung across his back, looking cool, like he was Bob Dylan or something. During the break, we'd all sit cross-legged in a circle on the floor singing *All I Really Want to*

Do, and *It Ain't Me Babe*, pretending we were the next Roger McGuinn or Joan Baez. That's what inspired me to buy my first guitar."

"And this 'Bob Dylan' guy taught you to play?"

"No way. He was into anti-war marches and all that. I was drawn to Detroit and Chicago Blues. I learned by listening to John Lee Hooker and Howlin' Wolf records that I borrowed from the local library. The woman on the desk must have thought I was an oddball; everyone else was into jazz at the time!" He closed his eyes, mind pictures of the past flashing like crazy movie scenes on fast forward.

Leanne grinned with satisfaction. "Have you ever dressed in girls' clothes, Colin?"

He pretended to look puzzled. "Only in a recurrent dream when I was a kid."

"What about the pink ribbon you wore this afternoon, wasn't that sort of dressing up?"

To give himself time to think, he flannelled his face, stood up, and stepped out of the bath. "You weren't meant to see that, Leanne, but I'm glad now you did. It was the result of a private moment earlier. I'd noticed the way your hair was tied up when you went out this morning. It was gorgeous. I guess I just wanted to be like you, sorry."

She dried his back and held his robe for him to slide his arms into. "The ribbon was lovely, I'm very touched by that. Now listen, wait in the living room until I call you, alright?"

33

He refilled their glasses and sat impatiently on the sofa towelling his hair. The suspense was excruciating.

"You can come through now, Colin."

Neatly laid out on her bed were dresses, jackets, shoes, embroidered flared jeans, lingerie, and much more. Plus, all the makeup, nail care, and hair care products needed for a convincing transformation.

"I know they'll all fit. Just say if it's not what you want, and I won't ever mention it again."

He was speechless, but his expression told her he was delighted.

She tugged at his towelling robe. "Let's have a look at you. If we're going to do this, it has to be right." After removing the robe, she turned him around, observing again that his body was unusually hairless. "Mmm ... nice!"

She touched his cheek. "And no facial hair. Wish my eyelashes were as long as yours. Lucky sod."

She took in his full lips, high cheekbones, his delicate dimpled chin. "Perfect!" She grabbed his hand. "You've got such slender fingers. And your shoulders are narrow, nicely rounded. The ultimate female figure!" She touched his chest. "Well, almost. But we can deal with that."

Reaching into a store bag, she produced a lightly padded lacy bra and matching panties. "We'll put these on you, then I'll do your hair."

"I don't know what to say, Leanne. This must have cost a small fortune!"

"Please don't be cross, I mentioned my thoughts about Colette to James. He suggested I buy it all as a thank you for the help you've been to both of us. You're the same size and height as me, so they wouldn't have been wasted if you'd said no."

"Did you think I'd refuse?"

"I hoped not, but I did wonder if you'd be too embarrassed to accept. James said for us to go shopping to complete your wardrobe when you feel confident enough, and he wants Colette to come out with us for dinner when he gets back."

Sitting him on her bed, she parted his hair on one side and set the front strands to fall in a seductive Françoise Hardy style. "Doing your hair and makeup yourself is easy once you get the hang of it. Just shout when you need help." After pinning his hair back, she got to work with foundation, blusher, eye shadow, lip gloss, and nail varnish.

He attempted a glance at the dressing table mirror behind him. "I'm beginning to enjoy this. I can't wait to see the new me."

"Keep still, will you? I'm trying to finish my masterpiece."

With the hairpins removed, the shock of hair fell naturally over one eye.

"Nearly done, sweetheart. We'll get you dressed, then you can take a look at yourself." White stiletto calf length boots zipped on, and a pretty lilac and white abstract patterned mini-dress fitting perfectly, she led her creation to the full-length mirror inside the

35

wardrobe door.

"Wow, that girl is stunning, I can't believe she's me. Thank you for understanding. I love you to bits!"

Leanne glanced at her bed. "Stunning, and very tempting."

A few steps along the hallway, and a circuit or two of the coffee table, Colette found it surprisingly easy to walk in heels.

Leanne was pleased with the combination she'd chosen. "That dress really suits you, and your legs look fab in those kinky boots. Talking of kinky, I was just wondering if your hair would look better sort of, Marianne Faithfull. What do you think?"

"With a fringe you mean?"

"Yeah, and a superstar boyfriend."

"Let's spend the night together."

"I bet you say that to all the girls, Colette."

"Superstar boyfriend you said … it's a Rolling Stones song!"

"Damn, I thought my luck had changed. Hey, you need some jewellery. Let's go shopping next Saturday."

"Next Saturday? You're having a laugh! I'm shaking like a frigging leaf just sitting here with you. What the hell would I be like wandering around Marks & Spencer, or Creasey's, on a busy bleeding Saturday?"

"Oh, come on, Colette. You're beautiful, your figure is perfect, and your voice is soft and not too deep. When you're not swearing, that is."

"Sorry, point taken. I'll think about it."

"It would be a crime to hide such a gorgeous creature from the world. We could make a day of it, yeah? Shopping in the morning, lunch, then finish off the afternoon in the Helmsman."

"The Helmsman! You're joking, right? Colin would be at home in that pub; it's usually full of local boating types. It's a bit rough, I don't think Colette would fit in."

"In at the deep end is what I say. Endure the Helmsman public bar on a Saturday afternoon, and you'll survive anything."

After consuming more wine, Colette warmed to the plan. The idea of spending a day shopping with Leanne was exciting. Now calm and relaxed, she sat quietly listening to Radio Caroline.

Leanne looked pensive. "There is something else, sweetheart."

"Go on...?"

"How will you feel if you're whistled at, or even chatted up by a man?"

Colette contemplated this for a moment, then grinned. "Flattered, I guess."

Privately, she gave this some more thought. As *Colin*, the idea of being with a man was inconceivable, but as *Colette*, the possibility was thrilling.

Chapter 4 - A cute blonde

"Are you coming out of your room for breakfast, Colin, or what?" Leanne shouted for the second time.

"Won't be long, and it's Colette, not Colin."

"Oh, that's great! But don't let your croissants get cold."

"I like cold croissants. Start without me if you're hungry."

Sitting at the balcony table, Leanne plunged the cafetière, poured herself a coffee, and lit a cigarette. So Colin needed no encouragement to be Colette today. When he appeared at the French doors, looking self-conscious, she clapped her hands in delight. "Wow, super cool. That white skirt and pink top look brill, and your hair has kept most of its styling, too."

"Thanks, I've kept the makeup light for daytime. Not that anyone will see it apart from you. It took three attempts to get it right, what do you think?"

"Looks good to me, girl. Now sit down and enjoy your breakfast."

While Colette washed the dishes, Leanne went through to her bedroom, re-appearing a few minutes later sunglasses raised above her hairline. "You'll find everything you need in here," she said, draping the strap of a leather handbag over Colette's shoulder. "Cash, tissues, and other bits, and here's a bracelet. Now go splash on some perfume. We're going out."

In her bedroom, Colette struggled with the bangle. "Where are we going?" she shouted, "I look a mess, I know I do … and what imbecile invented a bracelet that needs two hands to do up?"

38

Leanne smiled to herself. "You'll figure that out for yourself soon enough. But come here, and I'll do it." She also clasped a delicate gold necklace with a heart pendant under Colette's hair. Stepping back, she gave her a once over. "You're right, you do look like shit. Let's stay in."

Driving along pretty Guernsey lanes, Leanne eventually picked up the Vale Road to Halfway. Turning right, she followed the coast road towards St. Peter Port. "Not so bad, eh sweetheart?"

Colette checked her lipstick in the vanity mirror. "Um, feels different."

"Your lippy's fine, that's the third time you've looked since we left home … and for God's sake go easy on the Chanel, the car smells like a bloody bordello!"

Entering St. Peter Port, Leanne drove past the harbour, then turned left towards the castle and model yacht pond. She parked beside a trailered cabin cruiser near a boatyard. "Getting gracefully in and out of cars, wearing a skirt, needs practice."

Colette clutched at her arm. "We're getting out? I'm not sure about this."

"You need to take your first few public steps in a safe environment. I thought we'd stroll once round the pond, then drive across the island to Vazon Bay for coffee and something to eat."

"Um, right, I'll give it a go then. But if I get arrested for impersonating a hooker, you, Leanne Cameron, will end up in that sodding water!"

*

"How are you feeling?" Leanne asked as they made it back to the car.

"I thought everyone would be staring at me."

"You sound disappointed. You're nothing special to them, so why would they?"

"You're right. It's just me being paranoid."

"I don't know about you, sweetheart, but I'm ready for lunch."

Driving back along the Castle Esplanade, Leanne motioned to the back of the car. "Light me a cigarette, will you?"

Colette twisted round to retrieve Leanne's bag from the rear seat. "Sorry, I didn't bring any out with me."

Leanne smiled. "Don't worry, you can get some on the way to Vazon."

When the Mini turned right into the car park of a shop at the bottom of the Rohais hill, Colette began to feel apprehensive again. Why was Leanne grinning like that? Then it dawned on her. She must purchase the cigarettes herself. She patted her hair. "Now or never, I guess!"

Nervously, she pushed open the shop door. A bell clanged and a jovial looking middle-aged man appeared from a back room. "Forty Benson & Hedges please," she asked in her best feminine voice.

Taking two gold coloured packets from the cigarette shelf, the shopkeeper placed them on the counter in front of her. "That'll be four and tuppence, darling."

Blushing, she put the cigarettes in her bag and handed over a ten-shilling note.

The shopkeeper motioned towards the window at the car outside. "So, what are you two lovely young ladies doing out this way today?"

Colette nearly died. The last thing she wanted was to enter into a conversation with a stranger. "We're just going to Vazon Bay for lunch."

He handed her the change. "And a very nice day you've chosen for it too, darling."

Dropping the coins into her purse, she forced a smile and turned away, relieved that the encounter was over, yet elated she'd carried it off successfully. Just as she reached the door, it was opened from the outside by an attractive lad of about her age who stepped aside to allow her to pass. As she was getting into the car, she noticed him grinning from the shop doorway, and when he wolf-whistled at her unavoidable show of thigh, she smiled with embarrassment.

As they exited the car park, she slid back the window and blew the young man a kiss. Leanne laughed. "And there was me thinking you were a timid little thing. I bet that boy will have wet dreams about you tonight!"

The typical seaside café at Vazon Bay was not yet busy. As they chose a table overlooking the car park, the handful of customers paid no attention to them.

A plump young waitress took their order of hamburgers, chips, and coffee. Returning with the drinks, she said their food would be ready in a few minutes.

"How are your nerves?" Leanne whispered, so as not to be overheard by an elderly couple just settling at the next table.

"Getting there slowly, I think. I nearly had a fit going into that shop, but it helped my confidence."

When their meals arrived, they ate with leisurely enjoyment. There seemed no reason to hurry on this beautiful August Sunday.

The waitress took away the empty plates, and as Leanne lit a cigarette, a familiar figure in the car park caught her eye. "Hey, you're in luck girl, here comes wet dreams."

Colette followed Leanne's gaze. An old brown and cream Ford Prefect van had drawn up outside, and the boy from the shop was approaching the door.

"He must be besotted with you, Colette. But how on earth would he have known we were here?"

"The sodding shopkeeper … he asked where we were going, and like an idiot, I told him. Me and my big mouth, eh?"

The young man waited at the counter. Then, with mug in hand, he approached the girls. "May I share your table please, ladies?"

"Yes of course, please sit down," Leanne replied. "We're going soon anyway."

Choosing to take the seat beside Colette, the boy was unaware of the kick she aimed at Leanne under the table.

"Hi, I'm George Bisson. I saw you at the shop, remember? I've come to collect that kiss you blew me, but now I'm spoiled for choice. I didn't expect to be having coffee with two lovely sisters today."

"Flattery will get you everywhere, George. But we're not related. I'm Leanne, and this is my best friend, Colette … she's a bit shy."

While Leanne led the conversation, Colette studied George. She estimated him to be just under six feet tall. His straight black hair was quite long, and his faded blue jeans and a plain red tee shirt matched his casual demeanour. He said he lived with his mother in a house on the Catel Hill, close to the shop where she'd blown him the kiss.

George leaned back in his chair. "That's enough about me, what have you two been up to today?"

Leanne raised her eyebrows to Colette. Time she joined the conversation. "Our stroll around the model yacht pond was refreshing wasn't it?"

"Uh, yeah, it was exhilarating, too."

"Oh, really?" George said, "I work at the boatyard just by there."

The girls exchanged an awkward glance.

"What do you do?" he asked Colette, warmly.

"Um, we both work for the same company over at St. Sampson's, and share an apartment in La Vrangue." She hesitated, but George didn't inquire further.

Leanne gave Colette a surreptitious wink. "Look, I'll leave you two to it. I need to go to the ladies' room."

George was confident, talkative, and funny, and Colette discovered they shared the same tastes in music. She was intrigued when he told her that he owned an old cabin sloop that he kept on an inner harbour mooring at St. Peter Port. When he talked about his work at the boatyard, she warmed to him even more. He certainly knew his job.

George toyed with a spoon and studied the floral pattern on his coffee mug. "Look, I'm sorry if I seem a bit forward, but I'd like to see you again, Colette. Will you come out on a date with me? Or if you'd like to go sailing, I could take you out on *Bethany*. What do you say?"

A million reasons flooded into her head for saying no. Gently she took the spoon from between his fingers. "I'd love to, either or both."

"Can I call you?"

She jotted the telephone number for him on a napkin. "Don't ring before Wednesday. The phone is being moved and won't be back on until then."

Gulping back the last of his coffee, George said it was time he was going. He would ring early Wednesday evening, and if he couldn't get through, he would try again on Thursday. He leaned towards her, touched her cheek, and kissed her softly on the lips. Colette was speechless with surprise. "See you soon, I hope," he whispered, then headed for the door.

On the coast road home, she still hadn't said a word. Leanne glanced at her in concern. "Are you still thinking about that boy, sweetheart?"

Staring straight ahead, Colette remained silent.

"Well, you should have arranged to see him while you had the chance, you daft cow."

"I did, he's ringing on Wednesday, and he kissed me ... on the lips!"

Leanne did a double take. "What?"

Colette ignored the question. She couldn't stop thinking about George, remembering the way he'd briefly caressed her cheek, his touch sincere and gentle. The emotion of that kiss had been unfamiliar yet thrilling. She wanted more, but of course, there were dangers. How could she fake what she physically was not? How could she hide what she physically was? What would be his reaction when he found her out? Given time, he most surely would. But going out with him on a date, just once, what was the harm in that?

Parking in the garage, Leanne pointed at several sun loungers stacked next to a tool cupboard. "How about we take drinks out on the lawn and get sozzled in the sun?"

"Yeah, great idea, if I had something to wear for sunbathing that is ... which I don't!"

"Nor me, but if you open a bottle and get a tray ready, I'll get us something from the house."

Dressed for a Mediterranean beach, they took two reclining loungers from the garage and chose a spot on the lawn just below the worn patio flagstones. With suntan lotion applied, and the latest fashion magazines to read, they were soon soaking up the sun in the privacy of the shrub enclosed garden.

Pouring the last few drops of wine between them, Leanne got to her feet. "I'll fetch us something cold to drink. I could do with a shower, too. I won't be long."

Colette didn't hear the pick-up truck pull onto the gravel drive at the front of the house, nor did she hear footsteps approach across the flagstones. The first she knew, a man was standing over her. His deep voice and soft local accent interrupted her thoughts, making her spill her last drops of wine.

"Hello Miss," the voice repeated.

"Jesus Christ! ... You startled me."

"Not he." His eyes twinkled with wry humour. "I'm John Norman. I've brought some tools for the guys starting work tomorrow."

She squinted up at him, trying to focus on this attractive new arrival. Only a moment ago she was in that netherworld of not being awake but not being asleep either. She struggled to think of something friendly to say, but a smile and, "Hello, I'm Colette," was all she could manage.

When the silhouette moved round away from the sun, she saw that it belonged to a tall, slim young man dressed in working clothes and probably three or four years older than herself. His long brown curly hair and a well-trimmed beard added character to his sun-bronzed cheeks and hypnotic eyes.

"I was looking for Mrs Cameron. From the patio I thought you were she."

She glanced at the empty lounger. "Sorry to disappoint you, but as you can see…"

Holding the arm of her recliner to steady himself, he crouched down to her level. "Don't apologise, babe. I'm not heartbroken. Where else am I going to find a cute blonde on a Sunday afternoon?"

She floundered for a reply, relieved to see Leanne returning with iced orange juice. John's continued eye contact disturbed her though. It was almost as if he knew who she was. When he mentioned that he played lead guitar in a band called The Shades, she began to see him in a different light. This was her kind of guy. And when he invited them both to a party where his band was playing that evening, her love of live music overcame her shyness.

*

With just over an hour left to get ready, Colette opened her wardrobe door. Flared jeans with a white blouse and shoes would be comfortable and cool for the party. Applying her makeup a little more heavily than for the day, she chose electric blue eye-shadow, deep cherry lip gloss, and matching nail varnish for fingers and toes. She wouldn't score tonight, that wasn't the point, but she did want to look her best.

Dressed in flared Levi's and a short-sleeved pastel blue top that revealed an ample cleavage, Leanne came into her bedroom to do her hair.

Colette slipped her feet into white strappy high heels and transferred her cigarettes, lighter, and cash into an evening bag. She was ready to go, but feeling light-headed she slumped on her bed. Reality had kicked in. "I don't think I can do this."

Leanne put her arm around her. "Dolling up and going out for the evening is natural for me, sweetheart. But for you, it's a big step."

"All those people, Leanne! Someone's sure to sus me, and everyone will point and snigger. I couldn't cope with that."

"Do you think I'd put you in that position? But if you really can't face it, that's cool, we'll stay in. You're far more important to me than a night out."

"I do want to go, but I'm scared. What if I make a fool of myself?"

"I'll be there for you. I won't let it happen. Anyway, who gives a shit! You've got every right to be yourself. If anyone has a problem with you, it's their problem, not yours. You're better than them."

"If I feel uncomfortable, will you bring me home?"

"Yeah, course I will. So, come on girl, hold your head up high and flaunt yourself. We'll give the bastards a glamour shock and show them how to party with style!"

Chapter 5 - I just can't do this

Even with the fire doors open, entering the function room of the Fermain Tavern was like walking into an oven. A stifling atmosphere had built up during a sweltering day.

John Norman was setting up microphones, helped by a man with similar long hair and beard.

"You look like twins," Leanne shouted.

John swung round. "Hey, you made it. Grab a table. I'll be right with you. We're not twins. This is my cousin, Speedy. He has a passion for fast cars. Thinks he'll win the hill climb one day. Just might, too, the mad way he drives. Plays a cool bass, though."

A drum roll ending in a loud cymbal crash cut John short.

"Jesus, Danny! Can't a man have a sensible conversation with his new girlfriends?"

Danny grinned. "Don't be greedy, John. The groovy chick with the inviting cleavage is mine. I bet she has a fetish for ginger-haired drummers. I can tell by her sexy eyes."

John jumped down from the stage. "Guys, this is Leanne and Colette. They're good friends of mine so cut the crap and be nice to them, right? Thank Christ, here comes Tiny. Sodding late as usual."

Lugging a combination amplifier with one hand and a rectangular black flight case in the other, a blond curly haired young guy appeared at the fire doors. "Hi, John. Your new guitar is in the car. I've fixed the action. It should play fine now."

John dashed off to retrieve his electric acoustic guitar from Tiny's car. Five minutes later, he was playing a few chords, pronouncing the instrument felt great. He leaned it against the girls' table and returned to the stage to continue setting up his equipment.

Leanne nudged Colette. "Go on, you know you want to."

"No way, some musicians are picky about other people touching their instruments."

"Hey, John," Leanne shouted, "are you picky?"

"Picky? … What about?"

"Colette plays the guitar, and she wants to try out yours."

Colette shook her head. "No I don't!" she lied.

John gave her the thumbs up. "Sure, go ahead. It'll be a few minutes before we're ready up here anyway."

With feigned reluctance, she picked up the instrument. It felt good to hold, and as she checked the tuning, she was impressed with its strong resonance. She played a few random chords and a couple of verses from *The House of The Rising Sun*. Gaining confidence, she sang *Hi-Heel Sneakers*, adding a difficult riff in an instrumental verse. When she finished the song, she was embarrassed to hear a round of applause from the boys, who'd stopped what they were doing to listen. She put down the guitar before someone noticed she wasn't quite what she seemed, making a mental note to play songs that weren't quite so gender specific in future.

Danny, Speedy, and Tiny set about arranging the lighting. It wasn't yet completely dark, but in half an hour or so, the coloured lamps and spotlights would highlight the stage and provide some ambience in the room.

John came over to the girls' table. "You sure can play, babe, and sing too! Your voice is perfect for blues." Picking up his guitar, he began strumming a familiar chord sequence. Recognising it as the old Everly Brothers song, *Dream*, Colette couldn't resist singing along. Nodding with satisfaction, John gave her a knowing look and returned to the stage.

As the room filled, most people headed straight for the bar. Colette ducked her head and tried her best to be inconspicuous. A sly wink from Leanne made her smile. No-one was taking any notice of them.

The band started with *Gonna Send You Back to Walker,* and *Dimples.* A couple of traditional blues numbers, and some Rock and Roll. They seemed to be saving current pop songs for later in the evening.

Leanne drummed her fingers to the beat. "They're outstanding, Colette. John's wasted being a builder. He should be a rock star!"

"It's not that easy, Leanne. There are hundreds of local bands wishing for the big time, and just as many talented singers. It's not how good you are, it's who you know. In the case of girls, it's who you're sleeping with. The Shades are great though, just my kind of music."

"You ever played in a band?"

"Never had the chance. Doubt I'd have the confidence anyway."

"Talking about confidence, how are you feeling?"

"Bloody nervous when everyone came in, but I'm fine now."

"You look fabulous, girl. If anyone's eyeballing you, that's the only reason, yeah?"

Just before ten, John announced a short break. The stage lights dimmed, and the boys went to get food from the buffet. John and Danny brought heaped plates to share with the girls. While Leanne flirted with the ginger-haired drummer, Colette and John discussed the first set.

All too soon, Speedy and Tiny were back on the stage tinkering with the equipment and tuning guitars. Danny got up to join them, but when John stood up, he hesitated, catching Colette's eye. "See you soon, babe."

Just before eleven-thirty, the stage lights changed and the mood turned romantic. John placed his guitar in its stand, and the rest of the band went into *If I Fell,* sung by Tiny and Speedy in a convincing Lennon McCartney style.

When John leapt down from the stage, there was no time for Colette to protest. Not that she needed much persuading. Grabbing her hand, he led her on to the dance-floor. Hands on her hips, he swayed her to the rhythm.

She slipped her hands beneath his hair, her heart beating so strongly she thought he'd hear it. This closeness to a man like John, was indescribable. Resting her head on his shoulder, she began to relax. The smoochy music, combined with John stroking her hair, made all her inhibitions melt away. By the time the band went seamlessly into another slow Beatles number, she was trapped in a private world with him, the sensation exquisite.

The other couples on the dance-floor had ceased to exist. It was as if the band was playing just for them. When John's lips touched hers, the roughness of his beard sent shivers down her spine. His soft caress on her back ignited a passion within her she'd never experienced before. She drew him closer, desperate to show that, for this moment, she was his. His fingers stroked the nape of her neck and she moaned with pleasure. His urgent breaths on her cheek made her gasp. His tongue caressed her lips, pushing deeper into her mouth.

As *Yes It Is* slowed to an end, he grasped her hand and led her back towards her seat. They spotted Leanne waiting alone at her table. John gripped Colette's hand a little tighter. "This will be all right," he said, "trust me, babe."

He took her past the table, then up two steps onto the stage. Before Colette knew it, she was holding a microphone. John took another from its stand and held her close.

When the band played a familiar chord sequence, she knew what he'd planned. She sang the first verse of *Dream* with passion, and John sang the second verse, gazing into her eyes.

When the last verse drew to an end, he kissed her. "That was great!" he shouted over the applause. "You wanna do another number? The guitar you played is set up ready to go."

"Singing with you is one thing, John, but I've never played with a band before, I'll just make a fool of myself."

"No way, babe. You'll be fine. We'll do 'Sneakers.' Just harmonise the last line of each verse. You cool with that?"

While the boys played a few bluesy twelve-bars to fill in, John replaced the microphones in their stands. He handed her the guitar and made sure her hair wasn't caught under the wide leather strap.

Colette gazed out at the sea of expectant faces. On a stage in front of an audience, there was nowhere to hide. She strummed a chord, then turned down the volume. She'd sing as John had suggested, but the Shades line-up was already superb, without an additional guitar. Danny counted in, the party-goers crowded around the stage, and she did her best not to look nervous. With encouraging looks from Tiny and Speedy she eased the volume up, and by the end of the song her guitar was blending in with the others perfectly. She couldn't believe she was actually enjoying herself.

John gave best wishes to the girl whose party it was, and thanked everyone for being such a good crowd. Taking Colette's hand, he asked them to give her a big round of applause.

The band started playing again, this time a current hit by Cream. She wasn't sure of the chord sequence for *Strange Brew* but soon picked it up by watching Tiny.

During the repeated shouts for 'more, more, more' from the partygoers, she asked the boys if they knew a particular number that she'd love to sing now.

Dimming the stage lights, John left a single spotlight on full to add expression to her solo performance. Brightly lit, with the band in semi-darkness, she felt uncomfortable and very alone. The slow, sultry introduction began, and she counted under her breath. A cold dread gripped her and she faltered, missing her cue. She stepped back from the microphone and glanced at John, expecting a frown. But he was already playing an extended instrumental introduction, so natural, no-one would guess it wasn't part of a special arrangement. The cue came around again. She was ready. A nod from John and she hit the first note.

She sang The Casinos' recent hit, *Then You Can Tell Me Goodbye,* in a flawless Dusty Springfield style. Speedy and Tiny harmonised the refrain, and John improvised a soulful middle lead break. Couples smooched on the dance-floor as she performed the slow, sensuous number with all the feminine feelings she'd denied for so many years.

As if the venue owner was standing by the breakers with a chronometer, at the stroke of midnight, the lights went up in the hall. There were groans of disappointment from the crowd.

Preparing to leave, Leanne called Colette over. "We need to visit the ladies' room."

"You go ahead, I can wait 'til we get home."

"Not to pee, you stupid sod. I need to ask you something. It's what girls do."

Bemused, Colette picked up her bag and followed. "What's with the secrecy?"

"Danny and John want to come back to the apartment."

Colette's heartbeat quickened. "I didn't see that coming. What do you think?"

"I don't mind either way. I do like Danny a lot, but it's not about what I want, it's what the consequences might be for you."

"Yeah, thanks, but I'll be fine. John's a cool guy."

On the drive home, Colette slumped into day-dreaming, but Leanne seemed uneasy. "You do realise what's about to happen? You can't stash that in your wardrobe tonight, along with your clothes, then carry on tomorrow as Colin, like nothing's happened. John has more on his mind, and in his pants, than just snogging on the dance-floor. Are you sure this is what you want?"

Colette sat bolt upright. Trust Leanne to give her a wake-up call. "What have I done? What could I have done?"

"You could've said no, you idiot."

"It seemed surreal back there, almost a sort of game. But this is real life, isn't it!"

"Sure is, sweetheart. John will want sex. Are you ready for that?"

"What a frigging mess! What am I going to do?"

Leanne wrenched the wheel at a tight bend. "Well, the way I see it, you've got two choices."

"They'd better be good, or I'm in trouble."

"Right then, plan 'A' and the one I'd advise. Just be honest with John. Tell him the truth before it gets to the point of no return."

"Thanks a lot. I was on cloud nine, and you've just brought me back down to earth with a big thump."

"Plan 'B' then. You fake a period and relieve him another way, and if you need a 'how to' on that, I'm your expert!"

"Yeah, right, I've been a girl for a day, and already it's the wrong week! It'd be hilarious if it wasn't so bloody serious."

"Listen, Colette. When the boys arrive, I'll grab Danny and drag him into the living room. It'll give you a chance to talk to John in the kitchen, alright?"

While Leanne switched on a dim lamp and turned the radio on low, Colette put beer into the fridge and opened a bottle of wine.

When the boys arrived, Leanne whisked Danny away. But when Colette started chatting to John, he kissed her long and hard. "Not now, babe," he said, ushering her through to where the others were already starting to make out.

Pushing Danny down into the armchair, Leanne headed for the kitchen to get beer for the boys. She signalled Colette to join her. "You were quick, what did John say?"

"Piss all, he kissed me and shoved me in there with you two."

"Bugger, it looks like it's plan 'B' after all, sweetheart … you know what to do?"

Colette made a face. "I have a fairly good idea, but if it doesn't work out, I'll call my expert, yeah?"

"Stupid sod."

The girls placed beer and glasses on the coffee table, and the four began discussing the gig. Then conversation petered out. Leanne slipped to the floor to sit astride Danny, her hands on the rug above his shoulders, her long blonde curls tickling his face.

When John eased Colette back on the sofa, her heartbeat quickened the way it had on the dance-floor. She pulled him closer. He slung his leg across hers, and she felt his erection, hard against her thigh.

"There's something about you that tantalises the hell out of me, babe," he whispered, his fingers tracing a line from her neck up to her ear, then slowly downwards. "I need your touch, your lips, so bad it hurts."

She panted for his kiss, for his tongue against hers, but when his hand reached her waist and didn't stop there, she pushed him away, fighting back tears. This had to stop. Now.

"Sorry John, I can't, it's a girl thing." She rolled off the sofa, adjusting her clothes. She owed him more than a hollow lie. "Hell, no it isn't. I just can't do this!"

By the time she reached the kitchen, she was sobbing. Leanne appeared at her side to offer comfort, but Colette needed more than soothing words and hugs.

"How could I be so stupid? What the fuck was I doing, leading him on, then chickening out when it came to the serious bit?"

John put his head round the kitchen door, his deep eyes anxious and apologetic.

"It's not a good time," Leanne said, patting Colette's head on her shoulder. "Give her a few minutes, yeah?"

Colette sniffled. "It's alright. I need to talk to him anyway."

"Well, if you're sure." Leanne squeezed past John. "Just shout if you need me, right?"

Dabbing her eyes with a kitchen towel, Colette took a deep breath. "I've been bloody stupid. You must think I'm a prick teaser, leading you on then quitting like a selfish slut. I'm not like that, but I am different from other girls. I wanted to talk to you before we got as far as we did just now."

He gently lifted her chin. "I'm so sorry. I should've let you speak."

"It doesn't matter now. I like you a lot, and I wanted to be close to you, but I can't go all the way. There's no easy way to tell you this, John. I'm really…"

"A beautiful young woman, babe." He placed a finger on her lips. "I was here on Friday evening checking the scaffolding. I saw a young man on the balcony. His hair was the same length and colour as yours, and he was about the same height and age as you. Tonight, he's not here, but I believe he'll be back in the morning.

Chapter 6 - A butterfly necklace

At first, Colin was not at his best. But strong coffee before going to work, and more when he arrived, gradually cleared his head. From Leanne's pained expression, he guessed she also was suffering from too much alcohol and not enough sleep. He couldn't yet face up to the reality of last night, so her quiet mood was welcome. During the usual Monday morning staff meeting, he appreciated Bob and Frank's support for Leanne running the yard, and for himself as newly appointed foreman.

Climbing up onto the staging around *St. Terethe,* he stepped aboard. Swinging himself down into the main cabin, he sat calmly for a while, his trained eye surveying every joint, dowel, and varnished surface. Examining the removable galley plinth, he remembered the carpet fitter was coming on Wednesday to lay the flooring. After that, he could refit all the skirting, and the main cabin would be complete.

Later in the morning, Leanne joined him in the wheelhouse. "Sorry I didn't have coffee with you. It's been all go in the office. Typical first day in the job, eh?"

"Care to divulge the gory details? Hope your head feels better than mine."

"Not so bad as it was, and I'm sorry if I was irritable this morning. Damn, there goes the sodding telephone again. English and Guernsey for lunch and I'll reveal all."

Just a short walk from the yard, the English and Guernsey Arms had an excellent menu of home cooked food. Seated in a quiet alcove, they both ordered light ale and a bowl of Bean Jar; a traditional Guernsey dish of haricot beans and pigs' trotters, delicious with buttered French bread.

"In a way, this is a small celebration." Leanne offered Colin a cigarette. "The second cruiser is sold!"

"That's excellent news. Now we can order a new set of mouldings. Who's the buyer?"

"Richard Seabourne. James showed him over *St. Terethe* a couple of weeks ago, remember? His first deposit payment arrived in the post this morning."

"Local man, loaded, isn't he? Nice motor anyway."

"Don't be fooled by cars, Colin. Anyone with a bit of money can flaunt it with a Roller. But Mr Seabourne is the genuine article, a twenty-two-carat high flyer in finance."

The waitress placed two bowls, spoons, and a basket of bread on the table.

"Ah, I get it, he'll have influential rich friends, so we'll have to look after him, right?" He stubbed his cigarette in the ashtray, and ground black pepper onto his Bean Jar.

"We will, but that's not the end of it. Do you remember the actress who admired your work when the owner brought his friends to see *St. Terethe?*"

"Fat woman, works in the Rovers?"

"I wouldn't put it quite like that, and I don't think it was the pub.

But then, I never watched Corrie much anyway."

"Nor me, so what about her?"

"She was the one who called when I was talking to you on board *St. Terethe*. She wants an identical boat, and she's sending a cheque this week."

Colin smeared butter on his French bread. "When does she expect completion?"

"As soon after Christmas as we can. Sea trials February or March."

"Can't be done, Leanne ... no way."

"That's what I thought, so I called James. He said to set on another boatbuilder, someone who can do the fitting out to your high standard. I'll draft an ad this afternoon."

"Available boatbuilders on Guernsey are like hens' teeth. You may have to hire from the mainland."

"I'll try the local rag first. If that doesn't work, there's always the Exeter Star." She shared a secret smile with him. "It was lucky for me last time, sweetheart."

Back on-board *St. Terethe*, Colin worked on the control console to a stage where Frank could install the instrument panel, engine control levers, and helm gear. He next turned his attention to the marine radio housing; the parts of which he'd already cut from solid mahogany but not yet assembled. To avoid obstructing Frank in the wheelhouse, he decided to do this on a bench.

Now that his head was clearer, he could reflect on the previous day's events. Difficult to think as Colette while being Colin, but he knew he must get things straight in his head.

In many ways, George was like himself; a craftsman with an eye for the beauty of timber, and a love of boats. He had the same tastes in music, was funny and caring. Colette would be comfortable in his company. She would share with him the enjoyment of sailing and walks on the shore. He would be romantic, down to earth, and dependable. But George didn't know a crucial fact about her, and there was the problem.

On the other hand, John did know, but she couldn't rely on him. He'd enjoy a fling with her, but make no serious commitment. He wasn't the dependable kind. Dedicated to his music, he'd be shallow in any relationship. If she got emotionally involved, she'd undoubtedly get hurt.

But the most important question of all remained unanswered. Would Colette be satisfied with just a weekend existence? He doubted it.

That evening, while Leanne bathed, Colin made chicken curry. During the meal, they discussed the day's events, the good news about the new orders, and the placement of an advert for a new employee.

"I'll do the dishes, Leanne. You've had a hectic day. Why don't you chill out on the balcony?" He took their plates into the kitchen.

"No, I'm fine now. The soak was relaxing enough, and the curry was delicious. I'll run a bath for you though. There's something we've both been avoiding. We need to talk."

Neither of them now had any inhibitions about personal privacy. Chatting in the bathroom was becoming a favourite habit.

"How was yesterday for you, Colin?"

"It's been haunting me all day." He leaned forward for Leanne to scrub his back. "George, and the café at Vazon, and the party at the Fermain Tavern. But last night here in the apartment, with John, what a frigging nightmare that was."

"I've been thinking about that, too. I agree it was a mess, but try looking at it from a different angle. At least John knows about Colette and accepts her. Isn't that a good thing? Or are you so hurt that you want to put Colette back into her box?"

"It does hurt, but I couldn't go back now, even if I wanted to … and the fact is, I don't want to try." He stared at the ceiling. However exciting or traumatic the events of yesterday had been, his fate was now sealed. "Can I tell you my deepest thoughts?"

"Of course. Haven't we always been able to talk about things, no matter how personal?"

"Well, I know I'm stupid, and I know I'm probably unrealistic, but I have a strong desire to be..."

His words froze. Not because he was embarrassed, and not because he was afraid to say what was on his mind, but because he knew that once uttered, the sentence would change his life forever. A lifetime denial of his innermost feelings was about to be purged.

Leanne spoke softly. "To be what, sweetheart?"

Colin swallowed hard. It was now or never. "To be Colette all the time..."

For a tense moment, Leanne said nothing. Colin dared not look at her. It wasn't like her to go so quiet. Then her fingers caressed the nape of his neck, and he relaxed.

"First of all, I don't think you're stupid. As for unrealistic, it depends on what you want. I mean, are you saying you want to be Colette as she is now, as Colin physically but dressing in her clothes? Or do you eventually want to alter your body to become Colette completely?"

"I've thought about it for a long time. Until this weekend I wasn't sure it would be possible, but now I'm certain. I know that clothes and makeup are necessary props to create an illusion, but any girl needs those things to enhance her natural beauty and compliment her personality. No, those things alone are not enough. I have to be complete, it's the only way."

Again, Leanne fell silent. He sensed that she was trying hard to understand. But, how could she? "You can never know what it's like being me. You were born female. You can function as a woman in every way. Feel your breasts heave when you're aroused. Take a man into you in a natural way. And love, and make love, without question or guilt. You've never known what it's like to look at yourself in a mirror and despise your reflection. This weekend has made me realise that I can't go on denying who I am. I have to face up to reality and do something about it, before life becomes too much to bear."

Taking his hand as he stepped out of the bath, Leanne drew him close and hugged him. "It'll be a precarious journey, but I'll be there for you all the way, if you want me."

"I can't do this on my own, Leanne. I don't even know where to begin."

"Nor me, but how about here and now, eh? There'll be problems, but together we can overcome them. We have to make it work for you, sweetheart."

While Leanne brewed coffee, Colette put on a robe and stretched out on the sofa in the living room. She was exhausted, but somehow triumphant, the way a mountaineer must feel looking out from a summit. Still a helluva long way to go till journey's end, but she'd conquered the hardest bit.

Leanne placed a tray on the coffee table. "We need a plan. First of all, I'd suggest you don't go to work in the morning; it'll give me a chance to talk to the lads, and ring James."

"You'll come back for me at lunchtime?"

"I could, but 'Colette' has to get used to doing things for herself. You can take the bus to St. Sampson's, get off at the harbour office, and meet me outside the pub at twelve-thirty. We'll have lunch, then go to the yard, yes?"

Colette wondered how the staff at the English and Guernsey Arms would react if they recognised who she used to be. But what did it matter? She guessed she'd have to deal with many such situations from now on.

*

While she washed the breakfast dishes, Colette stared out of the kitchen window at nothing in particular. Colin had gone forever. She didn't feel sad, only a certain apprehension. Living on Guernsey and having friends who accepted her in her new life was one thing, but what would mum and dad think? She was sure her mum would quickly accept that her son was living as a girl; at an early age, she'd often treated Colin as a daughter. Dad would voice his disapproval, but mum would win him over.

Before leaving for work, Leanne had fetched faded jeans and an old pink tee shirt from the main house. Colette took them into her bedroom. They'd be perfect for work today, and with just a hint of makeup, the look would be fresh and natural.

Removing her robe, she opened her wardrobe for a hanger. Catching a glimpse of herself in the full-length mirror, she imagined her nipples and areolae adorning mounds of soft white flesh. But when her gaze moved further down, she grimaced at the constant reminder that she was not yet like other girls. Changing her physical sex would be a lengthy procedure. But in the end, she'd be as she always should have been. The prize would be worth the pain. Most people wouldn't understand, and some would harbour hatred and target her as an anomaly. A tough but necessary path lay ahead. She must find the courage to walk it.

Checking the bus timetable, she shielded her eyes from the bright sunshine and drank in the fragrance of late summer flowers wafting from gardens close-by. It was another beautiful island morning, a perfect day to start her new life. Spotting the old green Guernsey Railway Company single decker trundling along towards her, she drew her purse from an embroidered hessian shoulder bag that Leanne had given her, and took out the correct fare. In a friendly Guernsey accent, the driver bade her, "Good morning my love," as she dropped the coins into a concave tray next to the ticket machine.

Exchanging casual greetings with the three other passengers on board, she took a seat near the back, lit a cigarette, and wondered how she would feel entering the yard for the first time in her new gender. Bob and Frank were both laid-back guys with no strong views about anything. She felt sure they'd accept her. Her stop came into view and she refreshed her perfume, grabbing her bag to make her way to the front.

As she crossed the road, she glanced up at the harbour office clock, twelve-fifteen. Standing by the guardrail, she admired the colourful craft swinging lazily on their mooring buoys. They looked bright and cheerful now; a pleasing change from just a few weeks ago when their topsides were stained black with greasy slime from the Torrey Canyon oil spill. On the far side of the harbour, a dockside crane was busy unloading a small general cargo ship. Sacks hooked four at a time swung from its hold onto flatbed lorries; sawn timber in bundles so big that each made a single load. And on the quay, a neat row of new cars waited to be collected, their paintwork dulled by protective wax, big white numbers stencilled on their windscreens. An uneven stack of lobster pots, mixed up with fishing nets and cork floats littered the entrance to the public slipway where, in two weeks' time, *St. Terethe* would be lowered into the crystal-clear water. She heaved a sigh of delight. How lucky she was to live on such a beautiful island, with a good friend like Leanne, whom she spotted approaching the English and Guernsey pub.

Finding a window seat, they both ordered salads and a glass of light ale from a pretty young waitress who was too busy to take much notice of two more customers. Waiting for their order to arrive, they lit cigarettes, and discussed Leanne's morning at the yard.

"I bet you're itching to know how it went with the lads," Leanne said, as the waitress brought their meals.

Colette sprinkled vinaigrette on her tomatoes. "You could say that, yes. Come on, Leanne, don't piss about, did they throw up their hands in horror and threaten to resign?"

"No, not a bit of it. After my detailed explanation, they both said they'll be as supportive of Colette as they were of Colin. Result yes?"

"More of a relief really, but we've always got on well. That counts for something, I think."

"One thing though, and don't cry when they give it to you, but when they left the office, I saw them having a bit of a tête-à-tête. Frank came back in to tell me that Bob had gone to get you a birthday card."

"My birthday's in February. Don't they know that?"

"To them, Colette, today is your birthday. Just be grateful they're thinking of you. By the way, James sends his love and hopes all goes well for you. So there ya go, sorted!"

"Sorted it may be Leanne, but that doesn't stop me wondering where the hell this journey will lead."

"None of us knows what life has in store, sweetheart." Leanne caught hold of Colette's hand. "All we can do is try to make the right decisions at the right time, and not hurt too many people along the way. But there is one thing I can tell you about your immediate future."

"I knew there'd be a catch. Go on then, hit me with it."

"Well, you can hardly be the *foreman* now. So, from today you're officially the yard manager. And that must be the fastest promotion in history!"

"And a pay rise?"

"No, but we might manage a bonus on completion of each boat, how's that?"

Entering the big open doors, she followed Leanne to the office where Bob and Frank were waiting.

Not wanting the occasion to be too emotional, Leanne decided that light-hearted introductions would be best. "Bob, Frank, meet Colette ... Colette, meet Bob and Frank."

Colette was speechless, this was such a surreal situation.

From behind his back, Frank produced an envelope and a small gold-wrapped box tied with a pink ribbon. "I'm not one for making speeches and such, but Leanne has told us something of what lies behind the change that we see in you today."

Feeling her eyes welling, Colette was thankful to feel Leanne's arm tighten around her waist, as Frank continued.

"We, that is Bob and me, we wanted to let you know that you can count on our support, and we wish you every happiness for the future ... Colette."

When she opened the envelope, tears were already trickling down her cheeks. Over a multi-coloured cartoon of a dizzy female was written: '*What every girl should have on her birthday.*' Inside the card was another cartoon picture of a handsome man holding a dozen red roses. She pulled the bow on the gift, unfolded the gold wrapping, and opened a small jeweller's box revealing a delicate gold necklace with a butterfly pendant.

"We thought the butterfly would signify your transition into a beautiful young woman," Bob explained, "and the card is to mark your birthday as Colette."

Blushing, she thanked them both. Quite unexpectedly, they hugged her and formally welcomed her to the team. While she dabbed away her tears, the men diplomatically retreated to their work.

Leanne reassured her that now this bridge had been crossed, she could concentrate on building her new life.

That afternoon, she put the finishing touches to the radio housing, preparing to fit it into the wheelhouse the following morning. Smiling to herself, she was amused that Bob and Frank referred to her as Colette at all times, even though she'd told them that the usual 'Col' would be fine.

Arriving home, she was surprised to find that a note had been pushed under the door. But she guessed who it might be from. She hardly dared read it. Maybe he'd had a change of heart since Sunday. Her fingers trembled as she unfolded the note.

'Hi babe, sorry not in touch yesterday but very busy. Want to see you again, stay cool. John.'

*

Colette cleared dishes from the supper table. "So do you think he really wants to see me again, or do you think he's just being nice – you know, trying to spare my feelings?"

Leanne clattered dirty cutlery into a serving bowl. "For pity's sake, how many more times? If he was trying to spare your feelings, he wouldn't lie about wanting to see you again. It's a perfectly straightforward note from a guy who wants to sound you out on continuing a relationship. Just the right tone, not too pushy, but not evasive either. As two-line notes go, it's genius. So now could we stop discussing it and chill? I'm knackered, and I've got a full-on day tomorrow. After I take you to work and check the post, I've got the telephone engineer arriving here mid-morning."

Leanne picked up a magazine and was soon fast asleep in the

armchair. Still clutching John's note, Colette leaned her head back on the sofa and closed her eyes…

He's so good looking, he could have his pick of local island girls, and most of the young female holidaymakers, too. So why is he interested in me? On the other hand, is he homosexual? Come to that, am I a homosexual man? It's true that I'm attracted to men, but only as Colette. But then, as Colette, I'm attracted to women too. I've experienced sexual feelings towards both John and Leanne, so am I a bisexual woman? I long to change my physical sex to female. If I was a homosexual or bisexual man, would I want to do that? What if I found myself in an intimate situation with either a man or a woman? I can't yet function as a female sexually, so how would I deal with that?

Leanne stirred and opened her eyes. "Hot drink, or something stronger, sweetheart?"

"Um … coffee please, and biscuits if there are any."

"Yes madam, right away madam."

Colette listened to Leanne clattering around in the kitchen. She should go through and help, but she couldn't switch off her perplexing train of thought.

"Here we are. Chocolate digestives – our favourite." Leanne plonked her tray down on the coffee table and handed Colette a steaming mug. "Wonder if George will call tomorrow."

Colette looked blank. So much had happened since that kiss in the café, George had been relegated to the back burner. "Um, yes, I wonder."

"We're shopping at the weekend, remember?" Leanne held two biscuits together, chocolate to chocolate, and dunked them. "Now you're a working girl you'll need more clothes as well as accessories. If George calls, why don't you arrange to see him in town on Saturday? Or were you planning to meet him alone the first time?"

"I hadn't really thought about it. When he rings, I'll ask him. I've been thinking about John."

"You don't say."

Colette nibbled her biscuit. "You can be sarcastic if you like, but if I see John regularly, and I'm not saying I will, but if I do, he may, well, what I'm trying to say is..."

"Don't worry, I know what you mean. You think he's going to want sex, is that it?"

"Yeah, since his note it's been on my mind. Sunday was a disaster, but now he knows about me, he'll still probably want it in some way."

"And how do you feel about that, sweetheart?"

"To be honest Leanne, I'm nervous. Not because I don't want to do it, but I can't get the matter of sexuality figured out."

"Your sexuality?"

"Yes, and John's too."

"Maybe John's bisexual." Leanne dunked another two biscuits. "If so, do you need to know how he regards you? Surely, the fact that he desires you, shows his feelings towards you as a person and not a label. Can't you see him in the same way?"

"Guess you're right. It's people who matter, isn't it? Not their sexuality."

*

On Wednesday morning, making the best use of the time while Leanne was dealing with the telephone engineer, Colette called the marine radio company to let them know that *St. Terethe* was ready for the communication equipment to be installed. Updating the progress chart on the office wall, she noted that the carpet fitter was at work in the main cabin. Frank's installation of the helm gear was nearing completion, and Bob had reported that two more days should see the after cabin ready for a final coat of varnish.

While Bob made the coffee, Colette accepted Frank's kind offer to take one of the office chairs outside. She hid a smile when he remarked that stretching out on a nearby woodpile during morning breaks was not now appropriate for her.

Frank read out the advert in his morning newspaper. "Experienced boatbuilder required for fitting out new 35-foot fibreglass cabin cruisers."

Bob looked up. "Wouldn't be surprised if someone from our old yard next door applied. Not much call for traditional wooden boats anymore. Bloody glad I'm out of it."

Frank lowered his paper. "Me too. One of the lads was along first thing to borrow my roving iron. Seems his has mysteriously disappeared together with his adze and some other tools.

Heartbroken he was. All of it belonged to his old grandad. I think we both know who's behind it though, Bob."

"Graham Le Page! I'd put money on it, Frank. One of these days that bastard will go down for stealing, or worse, and I for one won't be sorry. He's a piece of shit."

Colette looked at Bob and Frank in turn. "One thing's for sure, he's only a labourer, so he won't apply for the job here. I wouldn't set him on anyway, even if he were skilled."

Frank looked thoughtful. "Look, Colette. I was going to see you in the office later, private like. But seeing as how Le Page's name has come up, there's something you ought to know."

She sat forward in her chair. She had a gut feeling that this news wasn't going to be good. "Go on, Frank."

"Well, according to the lad I just mentioned, it seems Le Page isn't too impressed with your gender change."

Bob threw down his cigarette and stamped on it. "Piss all to do with him!"

"I agree," Frank replied, "but we both know it was him and his brainless mates who did over those two fellas at the Spencer Davis concert last year. The place was crowded, but no-one saw a thing. They was only holding hands, poor sods. Live and let live I say. You need to be on your toes, Colette."

Bob nodded agreement. "No harm will come to you here lass, not with me and Frank looking out for you. Outside's a different matter, so be careful."

"Do me a favour, lads." She tried hard to hide her anxiety. "Don't mention this to Leanne. I'll break it to her gently tonight."

After an uneventful afternoon, the drive home took longer than usual. The heavens opened, and the first rain in over three weeks bounced heavily off the road causing the early evening traffic to slow to a crawl. It was noticeably cooler, too. A welcome respite from the recent heatwave.

Soon after dinner, an unfamiliar sound from the wall telephone in the kitchen startled them both. Colette ran to answer it.

"Hello, George. Yes, it went on today... Of course, how about Saturday?... You're working?... Oh, and maintenance on your own boat... We'll be in town and could meet you in the Helmsman, say, around three?... Looking forward to it."

She came back into the living room. "We're meeting George on Saturday, Leanne."

"Yes, I heard. That's what the serving hatch is for, didn't you know?"

"Daft sod. Changing the subject, do you know of a local villain called Graham Le Page? Works at the yard next door."

Leanne looked surprised. "James pointed him out to me ages ago. Nasty piece of work by all accounts, what about him?"

"Bastard's been shouting his mouth off about me, doesn't like anyone who doesn't fit with his idea of normality. He's been making threats too."

"Shit, that's all you need! What can we do about it?"

"Nothing directly. My guess is he's just trying to frighten me," she lied, "the lads are keeping their ears to the ground. We just need to be on our guard, that's all."

Chapter 7 - A real head turner

Tying her robe, Colette filled the kettle. While waiting for it to boil she enjoyed the garden view. After two days of constant rain, the sun had returned with a vengeance. Unhooking her favourite Flower Power mug from under the plate shelf, she heaped in a spoonful of instant coffee, poured the boiling water, and grimaced at evidence of the previous evening's overindulgence.

She stood by the French doors, mug in one hand, cigarette in the other.

Leanne lowered her Vogue magazine. "You look like I feel, Colette."

"There are three empty Chardonnay bottles in the kitchen. I can't believe we drank that much last night."

"You need something to soak up all that liquid then. Maybe we should go on the wagon for a few days, eh?" Leanne spread a generous scoop of marmalade onto cold buttered toast.

"Right now, it'd be easy to say yes. But when my head stops thumping, I'll probably need a hair of the dog." She stubbed out her cigarette and took the offered slice. "Great to see clear skies again. It'll be nice shopping today." She inhaled deeply. A unique, intoxicating aroma of freshness hung in the air. At times like this Guernsey was at its best. An absolute paradise, whose memory, like a drug, stayed in your blood forever. Wherever you might wander away from these shores, it would nag incessantly for your return.

Leanne yawned and flung down her magazine. "Shall we take a

minicab into town, what do you think?"

"Yeah, it would save you parking, and we both could have a drink, too."

"I'll order one for ten-thirty, is that alright?"

"Fine, what's the time now?"

"Don't trouble to turn round and look, sweetheart. You don't want to over-do it." Leanne stretched to look past Colette at the wall clock in the living room. "Nine-forty."

"Shit, I'd better get moving." Colette gulped down the last of her coffee and rushed off to the bathroom. The steamy vapour sharpened her sleep dulled senses. She turned her face to the shower spray, closed her eyes, and pictured the boatyard by the model yacht pond. George would be there, creating or repairing, or perhaps working in the chandlery. She wondered which of the boats moored in the inner harbour was his. She'd persuade Leanne to walk down there with her later to look.

Dolled up and ready to shop, the girls waited on the balcony for the cab to arrive.

Leanne checked her purse. "A bit of retail therapy will do us both good. No better way to spend a Saturday, eh?"

"It'll be busy in town, Leanne."

"You don't sound too enthusiastic. Cold feet?"

"Just a bit nervous, that's all."

"Hey, sweetheart. Head high and best foot forward, girl. You look a knockout, a real head turner. Loud and proud, that's what I say.

Let's go spend some serious money!"

Ten minutes later, looking almost like twins in heeled sandals, blue jeans, and tied front tops, the minicab dropped them by the Town Church.

Lingering at clothes and jewellery shops in the High Street was a temptation they found hard to resist, but a visit to the bank before it closed at midday was priority number one. Colette passed her 'pay cash' cheque under the mesh grille and waited. The cashier just stared; the cheque was in Colin's name. It was only when Leanne gave her a *'go on, make my day'* glare, that she counted the notes and passed them through without question.

Browsing the counter display of a jewellery shop in The Pollet, a gold bracelet with a butterfly design caught Colette's eye. It would complement the necklace given to her by Frank and Bob. But the matching earrings were for pierced ears only. Half an hour later, she stepped out of the shop with several items of jewellery, and gold studs gleaming in her ears.

Walking back up towards the High Street, Leanne paused at the top of a steep flight of stone steps that led down to the harbour. "I don't know about you, sweetheart, but all this shopping has made me hungry. Fancy an Italian? Luigi's is just opposite the waterfront. We could leave our bags at the cab office next door and book one to pick us up from the Helmsman later."

Colette grinned. "Great idea, Luigi's Capon Magro is delicious. While we're down by the harbour, could we look to see if George is on his boat?"

After checking their bags in, they dodged between several dithering hire cars to reach the slipway where they scanned each bobbing craft.

"There he is, I'm sure it's him." Colette pointed to a white carvel-built hull swinging lazily on a bright orange mooring buoy, a rowing dinghy alongside. "Look, George is in the cockpit. I hope he doesn't get sunburned. Bare chested is bloody sexy though."

Leanne smiled at Colette's enthusiasm. "You've really got the hots for him. Come on girl, I'll buy you a cold drink at Luigi's to cool you down."

*

The front door of The Helmsman was wedged open to combat the fug of beer and tobacco smoke inside. Catching sight of George on a high stool at the far end of the bar, Colette waved as he raised himself up over the crowd and beckoned them to join him. After the steep climb of Cornet Street, they were ready for throat numbing lager served in tall flared glasses, misted with condensation.

Colette ordered another round while Leanne, never one to ignore a jukebox, went off to select some records.

Colette gave George a shy smile. "*Bethany* looked wonderful when we saw you working on her earlier. I'd love to know more about her."

He grinned. "You've been spying on me, have you? Well, not counting her stubby bowsprit, she's a twenty-five-foot sailing sloop of American design. She was built in Weymouth thirty-five years ago, and other than a modern galley, her interior is mostly original."

"She sounds lovely, but why *Bethany?*"

He lowered his head. "She belonged to my father. He passed away two years ago. Bethany is my mother's name."

"I'm so sorry." She touched his wrist. "Now I know why that boat means so much to you."

"Dad taught me to sail. With mum, we'd spend every weekend, and all the summer holidays, exploring every inch of the Islands, and much of the French coast, too. *Bethany* is like part of the family. She has a charm that's hard to describe. You'd feel it yourself the instant you stepped on board."

"She's a labour of love in more ways than one isn't she, George?" She turned to look for Leanne. It sounded like he was about to suggest a sailing trip.

"Look, this is silly." He flipped a beer mat between his fingers. "Instead of me describing my boat, why don't you come and see her for yourself? The tides are right, so how about a run out tomorrow?"

A day's sailing was tempting, but being alone on a boat with George might not be a good idea. She played for time. "Well, I'm not doing anything, I don't think. I'll check with Leanne first, though. I wouldn't want to spoil anything she's arranged."

"No problem," he said, but she heard the disappointment in his voice. "Let's talk about you. You said you both work in St. Sampson's?"

Her first jukebox selection already playing, Leanne butted in. "We work at Cameron's. Being a boatbuilder you must have heard of them."

"I saw the advert. They must be doing well. Now I feel stupid going on about *Bethany* like that when you both work in a boatyard. Let me guess, you Leanne are the receptionist, and you Colette are the tea girl."

Leanne gave him a level look. "Actually, George, I own the company."

"Oh yeah?" He turned to Colette. "And I suppose you run the office."

She gave him a wry smile. "Well, let me put it this way. If you know someone as skilled as you who needs a job, tell them to come and see me, I'm the manager!"

"Um, changing the subject, what are you two doing tomorrow?" He flushed scarlet at what sounded like a leading question.

Colette took pity on him. "George wants me to go sailing with him, Leanne. I said I'd ask you first, in case you had something planned for us."

Leanne gave Colette a sly look. "Oh really? I'm sure I just heard him ask what *we* were doing tomorrow."

George looked defeated. "I'm sorry. Of course, I'd love to take you both out. The weather forecast is good, so why don't you bring lunch and meet me on Albert Pier at around ten?"

Colette began to feel excited at the prospect of some sailing. "I've never been to Sark. Any chance for tomorrow?"

He stammered with delight. "Sark is a beautiful island, Colette. The perfect place to picnic."

Leanne diplomatically struck up conversation with an elderly pipe smoking fisherman beside the bar. In exchange for frequent half pints of mild beer, he entertained her with spine-chilling tales of the dangerous waters around the Channel Islands, and his brave exploits in occupied wartime Guernsey. The Jukebox continued to play hits both old and new, and George stood close to Colette, an arm around her waist, his hand casually stroking her side.

Leanne abandoned her fisherman and returned to join them. "The cab will be here soon, Colette. It's almost half past five."

George looked reluctant to see them go. "Sorry I can't take you, I left the van at work, and it only has one passenger seat ... and anyway, I'm sure I've had too much to drink."

Colette thought for a moment. "George could come back to the apartment for a meal, couldn't he?"

"And we could all go out on the town later," Leanne added.

His face lit up. "Being stranded here, or being treated to dinner with two of the most gorgeous girls on Guernsey, that's a difficult decision. But if we're going out, I'll need some clean clothes from home."

*

Back in the apartment, Colette prepared vegetables for a stir-fry. Leanne plunged the cafetière, and George, unsure how to help, leaned against the kitchen door post.

Leanne handed George a coffee. "Best get this down you. It'll make you feel human again … sugar?"

"No sugar, just very black, but you two have had as much as me to drink. You must be feeling just as bad."

"Not us," Leanne replied, "we're used to it, and there's a heap of dead wine bottles in the garage to prove it!"

After taking a shower, and quite at home with a towel wrapped around his waist, George sat out on the balcony drinking a second strong black coffee.

Colette locked the bathroom door and removed her robe. Relaxing in a soft foam of scented bathwater, she thought about George. In the pub, they'd talked and laughed for over two hours. She'd told him as much about herself as she dared, slightly modifying some of the facts to fit her new life, but staying as close to the truth as she could. He was now aware she was a very competent boatbuilder who shared his love of traditional construction methods. At first, she felt pleased that he had no inkling of her physical sex. It seemed quite natural now to be female. But the more she thought about it, the more she reasoned that it would be better if he knew. That way he'd either accept her or not. As things were, she felt as if she was cheating him.

George had talked affectionately of his family but seemed not to have many close friends. She felt confident he'd be happy to have her as a friend, but would run a mile if she allowed him to get too involved before he discovered the truth.

She imagined herself approaching him on the balcony, making some piquant remark about the towel wrapped about his waist, then casually revealing her secret. He'd be shocked but agree to be friends. If only it were that easy.

Why should she have to tell him? Why should she have to tell anyone? Would just 'being friends' be enough? But was that what she wanted?

She imagined a different scene; she and George together in the privacy of her bedroom. She'd reveal her secret, then reassure him. Reassurance would turn to intimacy, his towel dropping to the floor. They would fall together onto the bed, his hands caressing her body but carefully avoiding 'that which must not be touched.' Feeling his arousal, she would respond to his urgency, providing relief.

"Are you all right in there, sweetheart?" Leanne shouted.

"Yes, of course." She hoped her feigned composure sounded authentic.

"Dinner's almost ready."

"Uh, be right out."

Hands shaking, she put on clean underwear, then wrapped a robe tightly around herself, a barrier against forbidden emotions. Taking her seat at the table, she remarked that the stir-fry looked delicious. She avoided eye contact with George in case he guessed at her bathroom fantasies.

Leanne gave her a searching look. "George was asking if we've been to the Royal Hotel. I said we hadn't, and he's wondering if it might be a possibility for later."

Colette chased a strip of red pepper round her plate with her fork. George's fork was poised while he waited for her response. She played for time. "It's just opposite the weighbridge isn't it?"

Leanne looked at George for more information.

"It is, and there's always live music on a Saturday. It's the King Bees tonight, mainly blues. You'll love them."

Leanne raised her eyebrows. "I'm up for that, how about you, Colette?"

"Um, yeah ... fine by me."

After ordering a minicab for eight-thirty, Leanne grabbed a robe from her bedroom and closed the bathroom door behind her.

Still uncomfortable around George, Colette cleared the table, then excused herself, suggesting he use the bathroom to change when Leanne was done.

By eight-fifteen, all three were ready to go.

George complimented Colette on her black mini-dress, a striking contrast to her blonde hair and blue eyes. He apologised for his casual jeans and sweater, and looked relieved when Leanne appeared wearing Levi's with delicate flowers embroidered around the wide bottoms, perfectly matching those on the collar of her denim shirt.

Seated in the back of the minicab, George reached out for Colette's hand. She felt uneasy but didn't pull away. By the time they arrived at their destination, she was much more relaxed. His calmness and warmth convinced her she was being foolish. Everyone had private fantasies, and that's all they were. No need to feel guilty.

She'd passed it often but had never set foot inside the Royal Hotel. It was a very grand establishment, but this was live music Saturday. She followed George and Leanne into the darkest, smokiest of rooms.

The loudness of the band covering a Yardbirds number made ordering drinks difficult, but the middle-aged woman behind the bar was adept at lip reading. Finding an empty table close to the small dance-floor, they settled down to enjoy the music. Conversation wasn't easy, but the King Bees solid beat and diverse repertoire, soon had them tapping their feet and singing along.

"Do you know him, Colette?" Leanne shouted over the music. "That singer keeps looking in our direction."

"I was thinking the same thing. He does seem familiar, the other lads too. Can't think where from, though."

Taking it in turns to pay for the drinks, they each made trips to the bar for rum and cokes. The evening progressed from relaxed to hazy. Leanne picked up with a young Irish lad who preferred to be called Paddy, while George appeared comfortable just being with Colette, drinking, smoking, and occasionally dancing.

He wasn't at all pushy. During the slow dances, he held her close but didn't attempt to kiss. He treated her as an equal, making no protest when she insisted on taking her turn to go to the bar. She noticed the way his long black hair sometimes fell forward from its centre parting, as if it was a defensive curtain across his face that allowed him to withdraw into a private world, peering out occasionally to see if it was safe outside.

"Four rums and two bottles of coke, please," Colette shouted for the second time.

The woman behind the bar took the offered one-pound note and nodded.

While Colette waited for her order, the singer announced a short break.

"That's a relief," the bar lady said, returning with the drinks and change on a tray. "It's easier to talk now. Are you on tonight, Colette?"

Another mystery, how on earth did she know her name. "No, I don't know the King Bees."

"Oh, that's a shame, my love. I saw you at my niece's party last Sunday. You'd go down well here."

"Hi gorgeous, I'm Bernard, Bernie to my friends, I was there too, we all were." The young singer handed a tray of empty pint glasses to the bar lady. "You were good, too good for the Shades! She was right, you would go down well here. How about it then?"

A few minutes chat with Bernie, and she discovered their mutual appreciation for female blues singers. She maybe should have persisted in her refusal to sing. Bernie's comment about her being too good for John's band was probably just an empty compliment. But partly through ego, partly through Bernie's persistence, and partly through drink, she accepted, agreeing to do two Ma Rainey songs.

Carrying the tray back to the table, she wondered what George's reaction would be. Should she ask, or tell him? Or would it be best not to say anything? Just do it and hope he would approve.

Only Leanne and Paddy were at the table. While she poured the coke evenly between four glasses, Paddy explained, in his rich Irish accent, that George was in the boys' room.

The band started playing again, but George still hadn't returned. She thought about the guitar she'd agreed to play, wishing she had a chance to check it out before going live. She would rise to the challenge and do her best. But where was George?

Then she spotted him, his hands on the shoulders of a petite brunette who kept snatching a glance in Colette's direction. The girl looked upset, but an embrace from George appeared to calm her.

Colette fought down jealousy. She'd only known the guy a few hours, so what the hell was this feeling? He had a private life that was none of her business. But who was the brunette? Perhaps an ex-girlfriend, or just someone he was fond of. As an islander, he would know most people of his age. He would have grown up with them and seen them around often.

George noticed her looking and rushed back to their table. "That was Jeanette!"

Colette pretended nonchalance. "Oh yeah? Friend of yours?"

"An ex ... honestly!" The curtains closed as he lowered his head in an apologetic movement, then cautiously peered out.

It was safe outside, but she couldn't help smiling at his 'caught stealing apples' look.

The King Bees came to the end of *Walkin' Blues;* a Robert Johnson number they'd played in a Muddy Waters style. "All right, we've got a real cool chick for ya now," Bernie shouted into a microphone. "Hey, c'mon Colette. We all wanna hear some more blues."

George's jaw dropped visibly.

"Sorry, I didn't have time to tell you," she shouted over the applause, "you were too busy with Jeanette."

The bar lady waved encouragement. Enjoying the adrenaline buzz, Colette stepped up onto the stage and into the bright lights.

To allow her to get used to the feel of the guitar, the band improvised some twelve-bar blues; the lead guitarist accentuating with a steel slide, and Bernie blowing a very expressive harp.

Whether it was her strong rendition of *See See Rider,* or because there was now a different sound, the atmosphere in the room had changed. Up there on the stage, she was committed to her music. Aware that the audience appreciated her talent, she was determined not to disappoint them.

Her second number was her own interpretation of *Prove It on Me Blues.* Unknown to many of the young people in this audience, for Colette this song had meaning.

Went out last night with a crowd of my friends.

They must have been women, 'cause I don't like no men.

Wear my clothes just like a fan, talk to gals just like any old man.

'Cause they say I do it, ain't nobody caught me.

Sure got to prove it on me.

She left the stage to tumultuous applause. George gave her an odd look and murmured 'Well done' but seemed subdued.

Just before eleven, to avoid the rush at the minicab office, Leanne said goodbye to a disappointed Paddy.

Their cab driver pulled up at the lower end of the Rohais. George thanked them both for a great evening and said he was looking forward to sailing the next day. He would take a bus into town and meet them as planned. He hadn't held Colette's hand during the journey, nor did he kiss her goodnight. With a heavy heart, she assumed he was unhappy with her. Perhaps she shouldn't have performed with the King Bees after all. Or was it something else?

Chapter 8 - I think I've killed him

"We've made good time, Colette. Only an hour and a quarter from the castle breakwater." George flicked a cigarette end overboard. "A steady south-westerly all the way. You must be my lucky charm."

"Perfect weather for sailing and *Bethany* handles beautifully." Colette kept her eye on a feature high up on the rocky shore of Little Sark that she'd chosen as a marker. "We'll be changing course soon, won't we?"

"We're well to the south of Brecqhou island, so bring her round a few degrees north and steer for the Pilcher monument. The foresail's in the way now, but you'll see it on the skyline, way up there on the cliff path after you bear away."

She pulled hard on the tiller and eased off the mainsheet. "Yes, I can see it! I wonder what it's there for."

"A very sad story. We'll climb up there later and pay our respects. Wait until you see clear water between Sark and Brecqhou, that's the Gouliot Passage, then ease off to broad reach. That'll take us into Havre Gosselin."

"Are we going in with the auxiliary engine, George?"

"Don't think we'll need to. With two of us working the boat, we can sail right in, then turn into the wind to lose headway. I've anchored here before. It's a sandy bottom, so when we're closer, I'll go forward, stow the headsail, and prepare the Danforth anchor. Wait for my signal to bring her sharply round to starboard, but watch out for mooring buoys on the landing steps side of the bay. We're still a fair way out, and I don't see any other boats, but if there's any danger I'll signal early, and we can start the engine to motor in."

"Yes, got all that. What about the mainsail?"

"Slack the sheet right off and let it luff. We may need to back it to set the anchor."

Leanne appeared at the companionway. "I can see the landing steps over there on the right, George. Now I know why you said we should bring the dinghy."

"You're still with us then." He stepped up onto the locker preparing to go forward. "I thought you'd gone dumb with fright down there in the cabin. We're running in at a fair pace, so hold on to something when we turn."

"I'm pulling back a bit," Colette shouted, as George made his way along the narrow side deck. "I don't want to get too close to the north side of the bay. I'll watch for your signal."

Raising a hand to show he understood, he untied the halyard from its mast cleat, payed it out, unhooked the hanks, and fed the foresail through the foredeck hatch. He unfastened the anchor from its blocks and made sure the rode would run out over the chain plate without snagging. Checking *Bethany's* position in the bay, he grabbed hold of the pulpit rail to steady himself and gave the signal to turn.

Pushing the tiller hard over, Colette watched the craggy shore of Havre Gosselin spin past the cabin top. She glanced behind. The dinghy was following *Bethany* round like a faithful puppy. Instinctively ducking as the boom swung towards the cockpit, she squinted at the masthead pennant, centred the helm, and looked ahead, just in time to see George lower the anchor.

George jumped back into the cockpit. "I think she's holding. We'll give her a few minutes to settle before going ashore. If anyone on the cliff path were watching that manoeuvre, they'd have admired our teamwork Colette. I know my dad would've been proud of us."

Leanne peered out from the cabin. "Bloody hell, I thought we'd never stop leaning over. My knuckles are still white! You two take a breather, and I'll bring coffee up in a couple of minutes."

While George furled the mainsail, Colette lowered fenders over the gunwale, made the dinghy fast alongside, and unlashed its oars from the cabin handrail.

Half an hour later, George rowed the girls over to the landing steps. Leaving the dinghy on a long painter, they started to climb.

"I knew it'd be steep." Leanne stopped to catch her breath. "But this is bloody ridiculous. You'd think someone would have the sense to put one or two benches along the way, wouldn't you?"

"It's a cliff path Leanne, what did you expect?" Colette took her arm. "Come on, not much further."

George put down the lunch basket and waited at the top of the rise for the girls to catch up. To give Leanne time to recover, he related the story of three local men and a London merchant by the name of Pilcher. They'd set out in an open sailing gig from Havre Gosselin to Guernsey one autumn evening, almost a hundred years ago. Caught in foul weather, the boat had foundered. Their bodies were washed up as far away as France and the Isle of Wight.

"Makes you respect the sea, doesn't it," Colette said.

"It sure does." His gaze shifted from the towering granite monument to the hazy shoreline of Guernsey seven miles to the west. "Many brave souls have lost their lives in these waters. Are you ready to go on, Leanne?"

The last half mile or so was much easier to cover, and after rounding a corner just past the Manor House, they were thankful to find a picnic area with shaded tables.

George watched Leanne spread a cloth and set three places with knives, forks, plates, condiments, and a jar of mayonnaise. "No wonder that sodding basket was heavy!"

"Just because we're eating outside, it doesn't mean we must let our standards slip." Leanne peeled foil away from individually wrapped, neatly cut sandwiches. "Ham and cheese with sweet pickle, or smoked salmon and apple. Just help yourself to salad. It's in a Tupperware container in the basket."

The sea air and the exhausting hike up the cliff path had given Colette an appetite, and the smoked salmon sandwiches were delicious. While the other two chatted like lifelong buddies, she thought about how distant George had been since leaving the Royal Hotel the previous night. Although at times he seemed ready to put his arm around her, his romantic attentiveness had vanished. Even Leanne had noticed.

"I'm off to buy postcards to send to the twins. I'll be several minutes, just enough time for you two to sort out whatever it is that's bugging you!" Leanne dropped her sunglasses from her hairline, picked up her bag, and strutted off like a woman on a mission.

"Wow, get her!" George looked like he'd been told to stand in the naughty corner.

"She does have a point though! Yesterday you were romantic, today you're nice. What's happened?"

"I don't know what you mean, Colette. We've had a great time today, haven't we?"

"When was the last time you kissed me? No, don't answer that. It was unfair, I'm sorry."

For several seconds George just stared at the ashtray, his long black hair falling forward. Then he looked up, hurt clearly visible in his eyes.

"When were you going to tell me? Today, tomorrow, never? Or am I just an accessory, like your jewellery and makeup?"

Colette threw a sandwich crust at a hopeful gull. "And there was me thinking my performance on stage last night had upset you! How pissing wrong could I be? I should have guessed the real reason and not turned up today. It would have saved you playing this awful charade."

"You just don't get it, do you! I've loved every minute being with you today. And I was very impressed and honoured to be with you last night. You're a fantastic singer, but I already knew before you went on stage."

98

"So why didn't you say something, George? I was going to tell you as soon as I could, but when have we been alone?"

"We're alone now, Colette."

"And you think I can tell you my life story in ten minutes? For me, it's enough that you know. In fact, it's a huge weight off my mind, and don't worry, I wouldn't have let you get too close if you know what I mean. I can see you're hurt, and I'm so very sorry about that, and if it helps, I'm hurt too. I like you a lot, more than a lot, and I don't want to lose you as a friend."

George shook his head. "I don't have so many friends that I can discard one just because she's different. I couldn't sleep last night for thinking about you. I have no idea why you've decided to be who you are, but you're an intelligent, rational person, so I figured you've had no choice, and I want to know more about that. Being with you today on *Bethany,* I've discovered that you're an incredible woman who I'd be foolish to dismiss as some sort of nutcase. I want us to be friends, close friends even, but right now I'm not sure I could get my head around an intimate relationship. I'm sorry."

Colette sighed. "I wish there was more time to explain how it is, but Leanne will be back in a minute. As much as I love her to bits, I want to continue this conversation between just us. There is one thing I do want to know, though … how did you find out?"

"You saw me talking to Jeanette last night. Her cousin's name is Tiny. He's the rhythm guitarist in the Shades. Guernsey is a very small island, Colette!"

They both knew a lot more needed to be said, but no time to say it. Leanne was heading their way.

"So, have you two stupid sods sorted yourselves out? Or do I have to bang your heads together?"

Colette glanced at George. "Let's just say we understand each other much better now."

Mainly downhill, the stroll back to the landing steps was much easier, and Leanne, possibly trying to prove a point, while leaving the two of them alone together, was some way ahead.

George looked thoughtful. "There's something I've been meaning to ask you, Colette. Yesterday, you mentioned that if I knew someone who wanted a job, they should come and see you. Were you serious?"

"With one cruiser launching the middle of September, another half completed, and a firm order for a third, we're pretty desperate. We've had no replies to the advert, and we must find another boatbuilder quickly. Do you know someone?"

"Yes, I might do, and I think he'd be interested if the terms are good."

"That's great! It'd be fitting out mainly. Is he experienced? Do you think he'd be prepared to work for such a new company as ours?"

"I can vouch for him. He's an excellent craftsman, and I know he would relish the challenge."

"This really is good news, George. Please tell him to come and see me as soon as he can."

"Why don't you tell him yourself?" He tried hard to keep a straight face.

"Don't play games! This is bloody serious. We need someone, like yesterday!"

"I'm not playing games. You can tell him yourself because he's walking beside you."

When it dawned on her that he was offering to fill the vacancy, she was delighted, but also sad. A working relationship would be bound to rule out anything that might have become more intimate. "I don't know what to say. I'm so relieved I could hug you. But I can't do that now."

He put down the lunch basket, turned towards her, and stroked a strand of hair away from her face. "How can I resist when you look at me with those big sad eyes?"

She put her arms around his waist and rested her head on his shoulder. When he pulled her close, she tried not to dissolve into tears. "Can I kiss you, George? Just this once for a memory to hold on to," she whispered.

"We're standing on what many people would describe as the most romantic and magical island in the world, Colette." He thumbed a tear from her cheek. "Do you really have to ask?"

Descending towards the last turn in the path, she felt like she was walking on air, and couldn't help gripping his hand a little tighter.

He stopped dead in his tracks and pointed to an old weather-beaten cabin cruiser in the bay. "Looks like trouble. That's Graham Le Page's boat, heap of junk. I'm surprised it's still afloat!"

"I know him, George. Nasty piece of work, always in some sort of trouble. He's a thicko labourer at the boatyard along the track from us."

"Come on Colette. We have to see if Leanne's all right. Oh, shit! But we have to get past those three first."

She recognised the fattest of the three thugs, blocking their path eighty yards or so ahead. "Graham Le Page himself, and two of his equally subhuman cohorts. What the fuck do we do now?"

George frowned. "Today is Sunday. With the pubs closed on Guernsey, they'll have been drinking on his boat all day. Their reflexes will be much slower than mine. There's no other way down, and no point in going up. I have to face them!"

"No! *We* must face them, George. But we'll have to be careful. I heard he carries a knife."

"I agree, but we have two more advantages over them. First, the high ground is ours, and second, he thinks we're scared."

"I am scared, George."

"Me too, but if we're to take him by surprise, he has to be convinced we're too scared to fight. I know the other two morons with him. They'll run if their brainless leader is taken down."

George's resolve was reassuring. "Sounds like you have a plan. It'd better be a good one. I'm shitting bricks!"

"Right, we'll walk down slowly. You hold on to me as if you're counting on me to protect you. I'll look like I'm afraid, and that won't be difficult!"

"Got that, go on."

"We stop a few feet from them, and I'll plead with him. While I'm doing that, surreptitiously select your rocks."

"Rocks? Yes, of course, we have weapons all around us!"

"But no further away than you can reach instantly. One round and smooth to fit in your hand, the other a good size for throwing. On my signal, grab your rocks and throw yours at the one on the right, I'll throw mine at the one on the left. As soon as they've left our hands, we both dive at Le Page. The smooth rock in your hand will increase your punching power. Are you ready, Colette?"

She took hold of his arm. "Not really, but we have no choice."

Hesitating every few yards for effect, they set off down the cliff path until they came to within throwing distance of Le Page and his henchmen.

"You're blocking our way, Le Page." George sounded as afraid as he could. "You look like you have a problem with me, but this isn't the time or place."

"Not with you Bisson, with him." Le Page drew a mean looking knife and pointed it at Colette. "He wants to be a girlie, does he? Well, I'm only too pleased to oblige. Sharpened it this morning special I did."

Colette flinched. George gripped her arm. "You're a bastard Le Page, a big man with a blade, eh? Why don't you put it down and settle this just between the two of us?"

"Walk away Bisson, pretend you don't know him. I never took you for a queer, but maybe I'll do for the two of you, eh? What do think lads?"

This was the chance George had been waiting for. Le Page had turned to his cohorts laughing, and for a few short seconds he took his eye off the game.

George signalled to Colette to pick up the rock she'd selected and deliver it swiftly to her target. Neither of the henchmen targets had reckoned on a boatbuilder's excellent eye for detail and distance.

Le Page's laughter stopped abruptly. His eyes opened wide with surprise as George's rock hit his right-hand man square in the face, blood spurting from a deep gash beside his nose. Hearing a sickening crack behind him, he turned sharply to see that Colette's rock had struck his other cohort on the side of the head, neatly removing part of his ear. What he failed to notice was that two angry rock throwers were on their way towards him.

George stumbled over the picnic basket, but Colette reached Le Page before he'd thought about raising his knife. With the force of her momentum and the speed of her weighted fist, she delivered a blow that felt like it would never stop sinking into his flabby gut.

Like a slow-motion film, Le Page's eyes bulged, his knife dropped, his legs gave way, the pale-yellow contents of his stomach exited like a grotesque fountain through his mouth, and long strands of silvery snot dribbled out of his nostrils. And when he slumped forward, face down into a stinking puddle of his own vomit, Colette stood back in horror.

"I think I've killed him!"

"If you've done for him, there'll be a lot of people on Guernsey in your debt." George picked up the knife, and none too gently kicked Le Page's head clear of the oozing puddle of spew. "But I can see him breathing, so no such luck."

Colette watched a snot bubble grow then deflate each time Le Page breathed. The sight made her queasy and she looked away. "Where are the others, George? I didn't see them take off, did you?"

"As soon as you made contact with fatso here, they both got to their feet and pissed off down the path. Just follow the trail of blood, and you'll find them. Oh shit, Leanne's down there. Come on Colette, run!"

Half running and half stumbling, closely followed by George with the basket, she descended the last steep section of the path towards the landing. But instead of two injured cowards, she found Leanne, looking pleased with herself, brandishing an oar like a medieval knight with a lance.

"You're not by any chance looking for two of Graham Le Page's literally bloody sidekicks, are you, Colette?" Leanne gave a satisfied smirk.

"Where are they, Leanne?" Colette gasped for breath. "And what the fuck happened here?"

"I'll tell you the story later, but right now you'll find two very frightened lads under that upturned dinghy at the bottom of the steps."

George shook his head in disbelief. "How the hell did you manage to imprison Le Page's two cohorts under a boat? Can't wait to find out, but right now I think we've had enough excitement for one day. Let's go home!"

Back on board, Colette secured the dinghy astern while George started the auxiliary engine. After weighing anchor, he steered *Bethany* through the Gouliot Passage.

Leanne handed George a mug, then sat down next to Colette on the opposite side of the cockpit. "I still think we should have dropped a big rock through their dinghy!"

"No way!" George replied. "It doesn't matter how much you hate someone, boats are sacred. And now we're heading home, tell us how those two morons ended up under that boat on the landing."

Leanne settled back on her seat. "I was well ahead of you two, and when I reached the steps, I saw Le Page and his sidekicks approaching in their dinghy. James had pointed him out once, so I knew he was a bad person." She shot a glance at Colette. "It was too late for me to go back up the path to warn you, so I hid behind an upended rowing boat by the safety rail. I heard one of the morons tell Le Page that Colette was definitely with you because he'd seen her on *Bethany* in St. Peter Port this morning." She gulped her coffee. "When they'd gone up the path, I decided to follow them and help you if I could, but I needed a weapon. There was a pair of oars by the boat I'd hidden behind, so I took one and started off up the hill. I hadn't gone far when I heard you, George, shouting at Le Page, then a scuffle, and his two sidekicks came running back down the path, streaming blood."

George interrupted. "We should be proud of Colette. She took on Le Page and felled him with one hate-filled punch to his disgusting belly!"

"Don't listen to him, Leanne. I was petrified, but we had to do something. Go on."

"Now here's the lucky bit, or unlucky, depending whose side you're on. I ran back down to the top of the steps, and I don't know how I thought about doing it, more of a reflex I suppose, but as they ran past me, I lowered the oar and tripped them. It was beautiful to watch. Head over heels, they tumbled down the steps and ended up crashing into the upended rowing boat. Then, with a satisfying thump, it fell over on top of them. All I had to do was wedge the second oar under the rail to trap them. I don't think you'll have any more trouble from those two arseholes!"

Colette looked at George. "I have a feeling we've not heard the last of Le Page, though."

"I think you're right. Oh, and by the way, did you tell Leanne the good news?"

"No, not yet. I wasn't sure after that scene up on the cliff path that you'd still want it."

"Of course I do. I certainly wouldn't let a bastard like Le Page make me change my mind."

"I'm so relieved." Colette touched his hand on the tiller. "I know you'll be supportive and help in any way you can."

Leanne clattered her mug down on the bench. "For God's sake, will someone please put me out of my sodding misery. What good news are you two imbeciles on about?"

Colette giggled. "George is coming to work at the yard."

"Well, thank Christ for that." Leanne gave a wicked grin. "I thought you were going to say you were pregnant!"

Chapter 9 - It's my first time

Leanne gripped the arms of her balcony chair. "You're doing my bloody head in! I just can't get through to you."

Tight-lipped, Colette stared at the elm tree, with gathering storm clouds above that exactly matched her mood. Leanne's questioning was an unwelcome intrusion, piercing the shroud of self-pity her own mind had created. "I'll deal with it," she snapped.

"You said that on Monday, you said it last night, and you're saying it again now, Colette!"

"I told you, I'll bloody deal with it!"

"When?"

"For fuck's sake, is this some sort of inquisition? I don't need it from you, Leanne. I don't need it from anyone, right!"

"None of my business, eh?"

"I didn't say that."

"George starting work at the yard next Monday then, is that it?"

"Give it a rest, Leanne … please!"

"We used to talk, sweetheart. What's wrong?"

"Nothing's wrong! Do I have to sit here with a stupid grin on my face just to please you?"

"It's Le Page. The shock is setting in."

"Jesus! Do you think I'd let that bastard get to me?"

"As it happens, yes, I do … he's getting to me anyway."

"Great! Then you go and wallow in your misery, and let me..."

"Listen, Colette. I've had enough of your shit! But if you need someone to take it out on, take it out on me. Just don't go around making everyone else's life a pissing misery. You've been unbearable at the yard since Monday morning, and it's not fair on the others."

"Fair? You don't know the meaning of fair, Leanne!" Colette sprang to her feet in a temper. "What's fucking fair for a freak like me?"

The sound of her bedroom door slamming was still echoing in the apartment when the kitchen telephone rang.

"It's John, for you … Colette, do you want him to call back later?"

"No! I'm coming out."

With an expression as black as her mood, she picked up the receiver. "Hello, John... Yes, I have, permanently now... I know you do... Next Saturday? Sorry, I can't... No, it isn't that, honestly... Because I'm really stressed... Oh, you heard, no I'm not hurt... Yes, it was, and two of his sidekicks... On Sark last Sunday… With George Bisson, do you know him?... Yes, he is a nice guy, and by the way, he knows... Tiny's cousin, Jeanette, told him... Yeah, another time then."

Colette slammed down the receiver and glared at the wall. "What—the—fuck—is—wrong—with—meee!" She pounded the countertop with her fist.

"Feel better now?"

"Don't start again, Leanne … please."

"I wasn't being sarcastic. You've vented your anger on me, and put John in his place. So, do you feel better now?"

Colette hesitated, then managed a smile. "Yeah, I do actually."

"I'm sorry I shouted at you, sweetheart."

"I deserved it."

"Go back to bed, and I'll bring you a hot drink."

"And biscuits?"

Colette folded back the duvet and crossed to the chest of drawers to rummage for her sexiest nightdress. A few dabs of Chanel No 5, fresh lipstick and her most seductive smile. She was more than ready for coffee and biscuits to arrive.

Leanne placed the tray on the dressing table and handed Colette the Flower Power mug. She sat on the side of the bed to sip her own drink. "Your mood, it was John, wasn't it?"

"Partly, I guess, but I didn't know how to deal with it."

"Can I say something? Or will you fly into a temper again?"

"I won't, I promise."

"I know it sounds daft, but I miss Colin. Don't get me wrong, Colette, you and me, well, we're good for each other, and you're fun to be with. But you're not funny anymore."

Colette grinned. "Like that bug eating the lettuce the first night you moved into the apartment. That was really funny, wasn't it?"

Leanne nodded. "Yeah, it was, and Colin's silly pirate hats, too!"

Colette stared at her mug, its psychedelic design the inspiration for one of Colin's songs that he'd been sure would be a hit one day.

"I miss him a bit too. I've changed, haven't I?"

"It was inevitable, sweetheart."

"You opened the box, Leanne."

"No going back, eh?"

"I can't go back, but it's taken time to come to terms with Colin's hang-ups."

"His lack of sexual feelings you mean?"

"He didn't lack sexual feelings, Leanne. He just couldn't satisfy them as Colin."

"I took him to bed because I wanted to be close to you, Colette, but you didn't respond."

"As Colin, it wouldn't have been right."

"And Colette didn't yet exist."

"I'm here now, Leanne."

"That sounds like an invitation."

"It is if you want it to be."

Leanne's dress fell silently to the floor. "You don't know how much I've wanted this, sweetheart."

Colette lifted the edge of the duvet. "Be gentle with me, please … it's my first time."

*

Colette's relationship with George was much cooler now he was on the team. Socially, they were close friends, but at the yard, it was mainly a working arrangement. Once or twice, in the privacy of *St. Terethe's* cabin, he'd made amorous advances and she'd responded eagerly, but he remained wary. He was certainly an asset to the business. Thanks to his expertise and enthusiasm, the yard schedule was so far ahead that Bob and Frank were now cracking on with the Seabourne boat.

She'd checked and re-checked her arrangements for the launch over the last few days, but it didn't stop her worrying. The blame would rest on her shoulders if things went wrong, and however much you checked in advance, things had the habit of going wrong at the last minute.

"I can collect the tractor and transport trailer after midday," George shouted, as he entered the workshop. "It all looks good for a three o'clock launch."

Placing the last hydraulic jack into position, Colette looked up. "That's great. We'll take the trailer stanchions off and back the flatbed under our frames. It'll be interesting to see if we got our sums right."

"No sign of James yet then?"

"He'll be here. He flew in last night but has some business to attend to before he comes to the yard. He and Leanne are staying in the main house until he goes back to Scotland at the weekend."

George drew her to one side and lowered his voice. "Be careful this afternoon. I've just seen Le Page in the plant hire compound with one of his wounded sidekicks who works there."

"Really? I heard fatso's been laid up for days."

"Word is, he's been shouting his big mouth off about revenge."

Colette thought of all their hours of careful preparation for the big day. "Shit, that's all we need, George ... any ideas?"

"I'd be surprised if he disrupts the launch. Too open, too many people."

"Be extra vigilant and tell the others. But don't mention it to Leanne. She has enough on her plate with the owner not being here."

"Owners don't usually miss their pride and joy being dunked in the wet stuff first time, Colette. What's up?"

"He called half an hour ago. Fog at Southampton airport, nothing flying, apparently. He asked for the launch to be put off until next week, but the tides say no."

"Pas de fête de champagne aujourd'hui ma chérie."

"What the...?"

"No champagne party today then. That's what my old grandma would say. She's French."

"We don't need the owner present to have a celebration, George. After all, it is our first boat."

"I'll leave here just before twelve and walk to the plant hire. Under the circumstances, I don't want to leave my van there when I pick up the tractor and trailer."

"Makes sense. It's going to be a long day, so go and grab a coffee. I've told the lads to take it easy. Not much they can do until you fetch the transport. I'll be in the office if anyone needs me."

Leanne was busy at the filing cabinet when Colette walked in. She took one look at her drawn face and guided her to a chair. "Sit down and relax for goodness sake. How's it going out in the madhouse?"

"Operation launch *St. Terethe* is underway, Leanne. Where's James? The lads are asking."

"He's wining and dining the bank manager at midday. Buggered if I know where he went first thing though. He's been bloody odd ever since he got here. Didn't even want me to pick him up from the airport, said he'd get a taxi."

"When's he going back?"

"Saturday morning. He's taking his Jaguar on the early boat, then driving up from Weymouth. Are you missing me already, sweetheart?"

Colette grinned. "Whatever made you think that?"

*

Checking her to do list for the umpteenth time, Colette looked down at the tide gauge again, then glanced up at the harbour office clock. Twelve-thirty, high water in exactly four hours. Sitting on a wall at the top of the slipway soothed her nerves, but Le Page's threat of revenge was a complication she didn't need. The sound of a tractor approaching brought her thoughts back to the job in hand. She waved her clipboard to let George know she was about to return to the yard.

She found the place in uproar. "The bastard!" Frank shouted, "just look at this. Good job we're not using the trailer stanchions."

George inspected the bolts Frank handed him. "Part sawn through and covered with grease. So that's what Le Page and his mate were doing in the plant hire yard. I say we cancel the launch until we know for sure what we're up against. What do you think, Colette?"

She glanced towards the office window. "James is here now, I'll put it to him. He won't be happy to have travelled down from Scotland for nothing though."

James was slouched in a chair mopping his brow with a handkerchief. From his ruddy complexion, Colette guessed he'd overindulged in lunchtime port. "What's the problem Coli... er, Colette? You've found Le Page's handiwork, haven't you?"

Leanne spun the telephone dial with a pencil. "I'm calling the plant hire company for a replacement trailer."

While she waited, Colette lit a cigarette. Her detailed plan for today was already falling apart. James' drunkenness could be yet another problem she'd have to deal with.

Leanne put down the receiver. "Not another suitable trailer available until next week. The manager's well pissed off though."

"There you are then." James squinted at Colette as if trying to bring her into focus. "Just get on with it, you don't want to miss the tide, do you?"

*

Colette watched *St. Terethe* make her way very slowly along the track to the main road. From this perspective, she looked smaller than when she was in the workshop. Seemingly unconcerned, James walked behind with Leanne, while Bob and Frank kept lookout for anything untoward. She'd accepted George's offer to park his van by the slipway with ropes and equipment in case of emergency, and the trailer had been checked over, as far as possible, for any further signs of sabotage. Beginning to feel more confident, she shouted over the tractor's engine noise, "Looks good so far, George. When we reach the main road, I'll signal when there's a gap in the traffic."

"Good idea. It'll look like I'm over cautious, but I want to turn this rig really slowly."

St. Terethe's short journey along the main road was accomplished without incident. With relief, Colette watched George reverse the trailer onto the slipway. Bob and Frank were ready to chock the wheels, and Leanne was retrieving coils of rope from George's van. Impatient with the slow progress, James had hurried ahead, keen to get to the English and Guernsey Arms before it closed.

"Hi babe, how's it going?"

"John! What are you doing here?"

"Heard on the grapevine that Le Page has something planned for today. Thought I'd stop by."

"Yeah, he cut some stanchion bolts. He obviously didn't know we're not using them. You staying for the launch?"

"I'll be here 'til your plastic gin palace is safely tied up at the wall, babe."

Taking the coils of rope from Leanne, Colette climbed a short ladder she'd fixed to the cradle and made them fast to cleats fore and aft. She signalled George to take the strain, then shouted for Bob and

Frank to remove the chocks and take hold of the lines she'd dropped over the side. Eyes over the stern, she watched the water creep closer as *St. Terethe* inched her way down the uneven surface of the old stone slipway. So far, so good.

Then with a jarring crunch, both offside trailer wheels parted company with their axles and skidded across the stone blocks. *St. Terethe* listed to starboard, her stern swinging sideways with a sickening screech.

Colette yelped as she fell heavily against the after-cabin hatch.

George fought frantically to stop the tractor from being dragged into the harbour wall.

Leanne screamed.

The cradle uprights creaked with the cruiser's weight now bearing down on one side.

Bob and Frank pulled hard on the lines, even though they both knew it was futile.

Colette grabbed hold of the cockpit coaming, crouched down and closed her eyes, waiting for *St. Terethe* to slam down onto its side. Nothing she could do now to prevent it.

Leanne knuckled her cheeks and gasped.

John grabbed a length of stout timber from beside some lobster pots, and sprinted down the slipway. He jammed the timber hard against the cradle, and put his shoulder to it.

The creaking ceased, the tractor stopped sliding, Leanne stood open-mouthed. John looked up to see Colette peering wide-eyed over the side, just as James lurched out of the pub, astonished to see the first cabin cruiser his company had built, skewed at a crazy angle across the slipway.

Bob and Frank shoved chocks under the remaining trailer wheels, while George, intent on helping John as he strained to hold the baulk of timber in place, dashed over to his van and returned with a box of tools. "Shit, that was quick thinking," he said, as he drove strong spikes into the cradle upright to prevent the wedged prop from sliding any further. "That should hold her for now. Let's get Colette down from the other side. This side doesn't look too clever."

John rubbed his bruised shoulder. "We both have an interest in looking after that little lady, don't we?"

"We're not rivals if that's what you think."

"I know that. You're a good man, George. Just keep her safe."

*

"I'm still not sure this is a good idea." George altered course to head between the channel markers at the entrance of Carteret harbour, thirty-five miles to the east of Guernsey.

Colette watched the gap widen as they approached the twin posts, one red and one green. "She floated off fine at high water. We both checked her thoroughly, and when Frank came back from the fuel station with Bob last night, he said she performed perfectly. Her hull, shafts, and steering are sound, and the engines don't miss a beat."

"I wasn't talking about *St. Terethe*. It's James I'm worried about. He's drunk again."

"I don't know what's wrong with him. He's changed since he went to Scotland. Leanne's in the forward cabin with him now. This shakedown trip to France isn't turning out to be much fun for her is it?"

Judging *St. Terethe* to be clear of the markers, George swung the wheel over to starboard. "That white Jaguar of his, it stands out doesn't it?"

"Only one that colour on the island, as far as I know."

"Thought so. Where did you say James went yesterday before the launch?"

"Leanne said he took the bank manager to lunch. She didn't know where he went before that."

George centred the wheel and checked the compass heading. "I know where he was. I saw that Jag of his in Collings Road on my way to work. Too busy to notice me though. All over each other they were."

"They?"

"Him and Liz Previn. I went to school with her. Not the sort of girl I'd want to associate with now though. Heard she was working away somewhere as a nanny."

"Oh, shit! For God's sake, George, don't tell Leanne until I've thought this through."

"Yeah, figured it out last night. She must have come back with James on Tuesday."

With fenders out and bow and stern lines secured, *St. Terethe* bumped gently against the harbour wall. Now they could both relax.

Leanne came into the wheelhouse with a tray of wine, "What happens now, George?"

"French customs are usually on the ball when a foreign boat arrives. I'll give it another few minutes, then drop by the Bureau du Port to register our arrival."

"Can I come with you? You speak French, and I need some shopping. I didn't have time to pack much for the trip."

"Up to Colette. She'll be the one left alone with your drunken husband, not me."

Colette saw Leanne wince and took her arm. "Sounds brutal, but George is right. He's wrecked, Leanne. I'm not sure it'd be wise for you to leave him in that state."

"He's sound asleep now. You'll keep an eye on him for me, won't you … please?"

Colette was reluctant, but Leanne sounded desperate. "After yesterday he's not my favourite person. But if you need provisions, go ahead. I'll check the engine oil levels and bilges while you're gone. Just don't hang about, alright?"

She watched George follow Leanne up the iron ladder onto the quay, then set about her tasks. Lifting the engine compartment hatches in the wheelhouse floor, she dipped each sump and noted in the log that the levels were correct. Stepping down into the main cabin, she sidestepped the fixed pedestal table, lifted the catches on the bilge access hatch and drew it aside. Replacing the cover, she noted that the bilges were dry. A noise behind her made her spin round. An untidy looking James stood at the forward cabin door, an unpleasant leer on his face.

"Get me a drink, there's a good girl. Scotch and soda, and make it a large one." He thrust an empty glass at her. "And where's that bloody wife of mine?"

"Leanne's shopping with George." Colette took the glass from him. "And you've had far too much to drink already."

James staggered forwards. "Who the hell do you think you are? Just remember who pays your wages. Now get me that bloody drink!"

She recoiled from his foul breath. "Go back to your bunk, James, please. You'll regret this when you've sobered up."

"You're so bloody smug aren't you, Colette. You think I don't know what's going on? You're shacked up with my wife, and now you're telling me I've had enough. Forget the drink. There's something else I want. You're about to find out what it is, you little slut."

She whipped round and made for the gap between the table and side seat. Before she could reach it, James grabbed her and threw her to the floor. His empty glass rolled under the table. She crawled towards the gap, but he dropped to his knees behind her, one hand tearing at the waistband of her jeans, the other pulling her hair so hard, she could barely scream. Pinioned to the floor, unable to move, she heard James spit, felt his hard, wet flesh pushing against her.

Terror made her determined. She managed to edge forward a few inches before James yanked her hair even harder and she squealed. The empty glass. Her only chance. Panic rising, she groped for it. With a grunt of frustration, James pushed harder. At last, her fingers closed on the glass. Summoning her last ounce of strength, she swung round, the glass shattering into razor-sharp shards against the side of James' head. He released his grip and fell back against the forward cabin door, hands on his face, blood oozing through his fingers.

She dragged herself past the table, scarcely noticing the gash on her own palm that left bloody prints on the carpet. Hauling herself upright, she pulled up her jeans with her uninjured hand, and stumbled into the wheelhouse, just as Leanne and George appeared at the top of the ladder.

"Can you take the shopping?" George lowered a cardboard box down towards her. "And help Leanne into the boat, will you?"

Colette's hand throbbed. She clenched her fingers to staunch the blood. Beyond tears, she fumbled to catch hold of the box, then struggled to help Leanne into the cockpit.

"Everything okay? How's James?"

The very sound of his name made Colette gag. "Not good, prepare yourself."

Leanne rushed through to the main cabin. Colette drew a few deep breaths and waited for the shit to hit the fan.

George stepped off the ladder. "Bloody hell, you look like death warmed up." He ushered her through to the wheelhouse. "I'll fetch some water from the galley."

Leaning against the control panel to steady herself, she winced as she unclenched her fingers, blood dripping onto the floor. "Leave it, George. Leanne's in there sorting James out. He's in a bad way."

He opened the first aid box on the bulkhead. "And so are you, Colette. That cut needs more than a band-aid. What happened?"

Glancing at the closed cabin door, she held out her hand for him to attend to. "A broken glass, that's all you need to know."

She watched him in silence while he cleaned the gash, too numb to register pain.

Leanne returned to the wheelhouse. "Well, that was a damned silly thing to do! Tripping over the forward cabin step is just about believable." She glanced at Colette's bandaged hand, then made eye contact. "But how he managed to fall onto a glass is beyond me." She turned to George. "I've dressed the wound, but I think we should get him back to Guernsey as soon as we can. He may need stitches. I'll brew coffee while you get the boat ready to leave." She shut the cabin door behind her.

George closed the first aid cabinet and turned towards Colette. "Something isn't right here. What really happened?"

"There's no point making a scene here in France. It'll keep 'til we get back."

James didn't appear again during the return journey, and Leanne only came into the wheelhouse once to bring hot drinks.

It was almost dark by the time they reached St. Sampson's and Colette gently nudged *St. Terethe's* fenders against the harbour wall. Home at last. "Can you make her fast George?" she shouted. But he was already scrambling onto the quay.

Jumping back on board, he stopped the engines and switched off the running lights. "Grab what you need, Colette, I'm giving you a lift home … and before you protest, I'm crashing on your sofa tonight. You need to sleep soundly without worrying that someone— he pointed to the cabin—might have another go at you."

*

Slamming the passenger door of George's van, Colette took a deep breath. James and Leanne's cars were both parked on the forecourt. "I'm going straight to the office. Time for a showdown I think."

"Be careful," George shouted after her. "I still don't know for sure what happened to you yesterday. But I'm angry enough to fix Mr bloody Cameron once and for all!"

Opening the office door, she was surprised to see only Leanne sitting at her desk. "Where's James?"

"He's sleeping it off. His wound wasn't as bad as I thought, and he was still drunk, so we stayed on board *St. Terethe* last night. I called the lads early this morning and told them to take the day off. If there's to be a scene, I don't want them involved."

"James tried to rape me."

"Thank God!"

"What?"

"You said he *tried* to rape you. I've been sick with worry, Colette. I thought he'd actually done it."

"You knew then."

"I guessed when I saw your bandaged hand. I'd seen the bloody handprints on the carpet. You want to share the details?"

Colette shuddered. "No … not right now."

"James is going back tomorrow morning. I'll keep him away from the house tonight."

"George is staying in the apartment until he knows for sure I'm safe."

"Does he know what James did?"

"I didn't tell him. He'd kill the bastard."

"I'd shed no tears."

Colette took a step towards the office window. "Shit! James is here, he's talking to George, and it doesn't look like a friendly chat."

Followed closely by Leanne, she reached the empty space where *St. Terethe* was constructed, just in time to pull George away. "Don't be stupid. He'll be gone tomorrow. Let it be."

"James said you've been sleeping with Leanne."

"Stay out of it, George," Leanne yelled. "It doesn't concern you."

George backed away in disbelief. "So it's true. What the fuck have I got myself into, Colette?"

"It's not like that, George. Leanne is…"

"Leanne set you up, Colette," James sneered. "Do you think I'd

126

go along with it if there wasn't something in it for me?"

Flushed with anger, she moved towards James, the dressing on his cheek a painful reminder of her ordeal. "What if I am sleeping with Leanne? You don't give a toss about her. You'd rather screw Liz Previn."

Leanne caught hold of Colette's arm. "Liz Previn is the twins' nanny. She's in Scotland." She looked at James. "…Isn't she?"

Colette held eye contact with James. "Not what I heard, Leanne. Where do you think this scumbag husband of yours was, early Wednesday morning?"

George stepped forward. "I saw the two of them all over each other in the Jag."

Voice shrill with fury, Leanne pushed Colette out of the way. "You're a bastard, James. You can sleep with your whore tonight." She slapped his face hard. "Come anywhere near me, and I'll cut your fucking balls off!" She stormed off back to the office.

Stunned, James turned and walked away.

"That's right James," Colette shouted after him, "go and tell Liz fucking Previn what you did to me yesterday. I'm sure the two of you will have a good laugh about it."

George had waited long enough for an explanation. "What exactly did he do?"

She hesitated, but it didn't matter now. "The bastard tried to rape me."

With Colette close on his heels, George caught up with James by his car. "You've ruined lives, yet you think you can walk away as if nothing's happened?"

"What's it to you?" James fumbled for his keys. "You're both fired. Get off my property."

Before Colette could intervene, George smashed his fist into James' face. "That's for what you did to Colette." He punched him again. "And that's for cheating on Leanne, you piece of shit."

James staggered back, blood pouring from his nose. When he finally slumped down onto the concrete, Colette kicked him hard in his gut. "And that, James fucking Cameron, is for what you did to me yesterday. Even so, you've got off lightly, you evil bastard!"

Chapter 10 – Puppet on a spring

"Sleep alright dear?"

"Like a log Mrs Bisson, thank you."

"I told you yesterday, Colette, call me Beth, everyone does. Coffee you have isn't it? Only instant I'm afraid. You're like my George, he doesn't drink tea, nor did his dad. Me, I can't do without my cuppa, 'specially in the mornings. Nice bit of bacon for breakfast. You do eat eggs, don't you? Course you do. George loves his bacon, so did his dad. I've done some fried bread too. By the looks of you a bit of fried bread won't hurt, thin as a rake you are. George's dad always said I was cuddly, I do miss him. Lovely hair."

"George's dad had lovely hair, Beth?"

"No, not him, you. You've got lovely hair dear, reminds me of that French singer, what's her name, saw her on the telly just the other night. No, don't tell me, I'll think of it in a minute. Now, what was her name, blonde girl, just like you. No, it's gone. You'll have to tell me."

"Françoise Hardy?"

"No, no, not her. French girl dear. Puppet on a spring or something."

Colette hid a smile. "You mean Sandie Shaw. She's not French, lovely singer though, Mrs Bisson. I like her very much. I'm flattered you think I look like her."

"Did I say she was French? Ah well, George's dad always said I got things in a muddle. You'll get used to me. Call me Beth dear, and how's that hand of yours?"

"Three stitches at the hospital yesterday. The doctor said I should have gone sooner. George insisted on taking me."

"That's my George, just like his dad, always doing good turns. He's a good boy is George. Doesn't often bring girls home. Come to think of it, he's never brought a girl home at all. Not like his cousin Jean. Lovely girl."

"Um, your niece, Jean, takes girls home?"

"No, course not, whatever gave you that idea? Jean Pierre, he's my nephew. Never could say Jean the French way. George's dad could. He was half French."

"Oh, sorry. You said 'lovely girl' I thought…"

"No, not him. You dear, you're a lovely girl. I expected you to be older, you being George's boss and all."

"I *was* George's boss. I don't know what…"

"Oh, you'll be alright, don't you worry. You can stay with me as long as you like. A bit of female company is just what I need. You too Colette, all them men you work with."

"Morning Ma, do I smell bacon?"

"It's Saturday, George. You always have bacon on a Saturday. Been having a right old chinwag me an' Colette. Sit down, son. I'll bring your breakfasts."

"What are we going to do, George?" Colette whispered. "Your mum said I could stay here. I've got enough money to tide me over, but I can't think any further than that."

"Mum always takes the bus into town on Saturdays. We'll sort something out then."

*

Slumped at the kitchen table in the main house, James looked haggard and hungover, but Leanne was determined not to let him off the hook. "If you think you're coming back here, you've another think coming."

"How many times do I have to say sorry, Leanne? I was drunk. You know what I'm like when I've had too much. I'll apologise to Colette."

"You raped her, James."

"No, that's a lie."

"As good as then. It wasn't supposed to be like that. We always said it had to be consensual. Anyway, you knew the plan had changed. Colette was just getting her head together. God knows where she is now. And what's with you and Liz? You broke our golden rule and didn't tell me."

"It's serious, Leanne. I never thought I'd have to say that to you."

"Shit! Here we go again. I'll pour you a coffee. You look like you need one. Didn't that hotel have a bathroom?"

"Checked out first thing. I had to talk to you."

"Well, you've missed the early boat. Liz will be frantic. Have you called her?"

"I picked her up on the way here. She's waiting in the car."

"You mean she still wants you with your face in a mess?"

131

"It'll heal. Bloody hurts though, and I think a rib's broken."

"You deserved it, and what the fuck were you doing firing my two best boatbuilders?"

"Your two best boatbuilders? It's my company, don't forget."

"The boatyard may be in your name, James. But it's my money went into it. You own nothing. Not even the house."

"As your husband, I own half."

"You're forgetting the prenuptial you made me sign. Bet you wouldn't have done that if you'd known my grandad was planning to leave me his fortune. You're a loser James. Even your ad agency is going down the sodding toilet."

"It'll pick up now we've got the Glencallan distillery campaign, you'll see."

"Whisky! That says it all about you."

"What are we going to do, Leanne?"

"I don't know … are you really serious about Liz?"

"She says she loves me."

"She's eighteen, and you're forty-five! Think that stands a chance?"

"She's nineteen. It was her birthday yesterday. I brought her back to see her family."

"You could have told me."

"We went to Jersey for a couple of days, hotel in St. Helier. You'd have sussed when we came in on the wrong plane."

"And you lied to your parents, too?"

"Told them Liz was visiting friends in London."

"What about the twins?"

"Happy with their grandparents. They started the new school last week."

"I didn't mean that. How are they with Liz?"

"They don't call her Mum, if that's what you mean."

"Fetch her in here, I want to talk to her."

"No way, I know you. You'll tear her apart!"

"Just do it, James."

*

Colette watched George idly turning his lighter between his fingers. "What a mess, I never thought it would end like this. What will you do?"

"I'll go and see my old boss. Maybe he'll give me my job back."

"He'd be stupid not to."

"Shame though, I really thought Cameron's was a good move. What about you?"

"Yeah, what about me. I'll see the summer out on Guernsey, then back to the mainland."

"As Colette?"

"Doubt it. I'll maybe give my friend Sam a call. She'd put me up as Colette. I'll see how it pans out."

George touched her hand. "Good times though."

Colette shrugged. "While it lasted."

He hauled her to her feet. "Come on. I'll take you to the

apartment. Best do it now, get it over with, eh?"

"I'll need some bags. I only had a holdall when I arrived. We'll collect our tools from the yard, too. I still have a key."

*

"Out James. I want to talk to Liz on her own."

"Say what you need to say, I'm not leaving."

"Out … Now!"

"Shit! What's the matter with you, Leanne? Ok, ok, I'm going. I'll be in the hall, Liz. If I hear you shout, I'll be back in like a shot."

"Look, Mrs Cameron, I don't know what he's told you but…"

"I didn't ask him to bring you in here so I could listen to your crap. Let's get one thing straight. This is my house, James is my husband, and the twins are my kids, right?"

"That's three things, Mrs Cameron."

"Very funny. You're only nineteen, Liz. James is a lot older than you. How long do you think it'll be before you get tired of him and want someone your own age?"

"He's older than you too, Mrs Cameron."

"Not by twenty-six bloody years he isn't."

"Um that's um…"

"He's forty-five Liz! He probably told you he's younger. It wouldn't be the first time."

"Yeah, he did. But it don't matter do it? When two people love each other, what's a few years?"

"And do you love him?"

"Why are you asking me these things, Mrs Cameron? I don't understand."

"Give me strength … Love! Not just screwing, although you've probably done plenty of that. Love is the feeling you get when you've met the person you want to spend your life with. Love, yeah? So, do you love him?"

"I do, yes."

"Well done! That wasn't so difficult, was it? Now, if I told you that I don't love James anymore, what would you say?"

"What are you getting at, Mrs Cameron?"

"I'm telling you he's yours, Liz. There's just one condition. Stop me from seeing my kids whenever I want, and I'll make your life a fucking misery. Got that?"

She opened the hallway door. "That's it then, James. I'll pack your things and send them on. I hope you'll both be happy … and for some stupid reason, I actually mean that."

"What about the yard, Leanne? I can't afford to let that go bust. It's all the income I have until the agency picks up."

"You'll get your cut. Just stay away, that's all."

Leanne stood under the elm tree and watched James' Jaguar disappear through the tall wrought iron gates. Locking the main house door, she crossed the courtyard and climbed the apartment steps. The kitchen seemed so empty now. She remembered the day she'd moved in, Colin stirring a pot on the hob. *It's been three bloody days, Leanne. I've been going nuts.*

She opened Colette's bedroom door and smiled at the sight of one of Colin's daft pirate hats on the dressing table. She picked up the ribbon coiled beside it and held it to her cheek. *I love you to bits, Colin, pink ribbon and all.* Crossing to the wardrobe, she swished her hand through Colette's dresses. The motion stirred a sweet wave of perfume. She'd helped Colette choose that fragrance on an innocent girly shopping trip.

She caught a glimpse of herself in the full-length mirror on the wardrobe door. A stranger's face stared back. How had she got to this, wounding the woman she loved for the sake of some kinky game that got out of hand? Her reflection seemed to mock her. *What's fucking fair for a freak like me, eh?* She twisted Colin's fragile scrap of ribbon between her fingers. "Forgive me, sweetheart. I'm here for you," she whispered. But nobody heard.

At the sound of a vehicle pulling into the courtyard, she rushed to the balcony to see if it was Colette. Anger jostled with relief. "Where the hell have you been? I've been worried stiff."

Colette held up the bags. "I've come to collect my stuff."

"Just get up here the two of you ... and leave those sodding bags in the van."

*

Gripping the steering wheel of his Jaguar, his swollen face set in a permanent scowl, James pulled away from the curb outside the travel agency. "I still can't believe it, Liz. She's never done this before. I've always said sorry, several times usually, and it's been alright.

But I think she really means it this time!"

"You've still got me James, and we do love each other, don't we?"

"She'll come round, no worries. Give her a couple of weeks."

Liz rummaged in her bag. "So, what do we do now? I need to get to a chemist."

"There's no time. We're on the afternoon ferry. The ticket clerk let me use the phone. I've booked us a hotel room in Weymouth."

"You don't understand, James. This is urgent. I need to, you know, sort myself out."

"I don't bloody know, Liz. What's the matter with you?"

"I just started my period."

James clenched his teeth. "Oh, Shit!"

*

"All I'm asking is that you come back to work, George. I'll make it up to you somehow."

"If that husband of yours comes anywhere near Colette or me, he'll have more than just a broken nose next time, Leanne."

"He won't. He knows what he'll lose if he does."

"I'll be off then. You ok staying here, Colette?"

"My jacket's in the van. I'll come down with you."

From the courtyard, she spotted Leanne on the balcony above, watching. Why couldn't she give them five minutes privacy? She drew George out of sight, towards the shelter of the garage wall.

"Thank your mum for me, she's lovely. Tell her sorry I'm not coming back. I'll stay in touch."

"Mum in a million, but all sons and daughters say that, don't they?" He stepped away looking uneasy. "I'll be getting along now, see you on Monday."

"I was hoping we could go out tonight, just the two of us, see a band or something, a restaurant if you like. My treat."

George ducked his head, his hair screening his face. "I can't Colette," he mumbled, "I already promised someone. I'd have put her off if you'd stayed with mum and me."

"Jeanette?"

"Yeah, you knew, didn't you?"

Back in the apartment, Colette headed for her room to hide the hurt in her eyes. She couldn't disguise her feelings that easily. Leanne slipped an arm round her waist. "I'll cook dinner tonight, sweetheart. A glass or two of wine and an early night, eh? Wear that sexy nightdress for me again. What do you say?"

"Dinner and wine are fine, Leanne. But I'm sleeping on my own from now on. Sorry."

PART TWO

Chapter 11 - A Dusty Springfield number

Leanne reversed her Mini into a narrow space next to the fire doors at the Fermain Tavern. "That's one of the benefits of having a small car, Colette. Grab the gifts from the back seat. You've got their cards, haven't you?"

"I put them in the bag with the presents. I still can't get over the fact that George's birthday is on the same day as his mum's. What are the chances of that?"

"Buggered if I know. But the fifth of November is easy to remember, and a Sunday this year. It was a pleasure to arrange this party for him as a thank you for coming back to work. And his mum is a one-off, isn't she?"

"Yeah, she's lovely. You were lucky to book John's band. I'm looking forward to playing with the Shades again."

"Danny had better keep his hands to himself. I'm off men since that sodding husband of mine pissed off with the nanny ... and what he did to you!"

Colette checked the birthday cards were still in the bag. "It was nearly two months ago. I still have the nightmares."

"Come on, sweetheart. Remember what we used to say? Loud and proud, let's show them how to party!"

They hurried across the dimly lit car park, the impact of entering the venue looking fabulous outweighing the need for coats.

Just inside the function room door, Leanne handed the bag to

139

George's mum who was waiting in front of a table piled high with wrapped gifts. "Just a small something for you and George from Colette and me, Mrs Bisson. Happy birthday."

"Call me Beth dear, everyone does, and you shouldn't have brought presents. Putting on this party for my boy and me is plenty enough. I don't know how to thank you. No-one's ever done this before, not even George's dad. You'd have loved him, Mrs Cameron. Just like you he was."

"Really? A blonde bombshell, was he? And please call me Leanne."

"No, no, he wasn't blonde, Mrs Cameron. But he did have most of his own hair. More of a grey it was when he went."

"Sorry Beth, you said he was like me."

"Always smiling. You've got a lovely smile, Leanne. Catch your death in that dress, couldn't you find one in your size? You should go down to Creasey's on a Saturday, get yourself something warm. Purple suits you, so you got that right. And here's Colette, you do look lovely dear. I always say black's not just for funerals. A bit on the short side for that, but it'd only be the mourners who'd notice, and the priest of course if it was church."

As Leanne moved along to talk to George, Colette stepped forward trying not to chuckle. "Happy birthday, Beth. Looks like you've got loads of presents between you."

"Soap and talc for me and bottles for George. When you get to my age, you can tell by the weight and shape." She peered inside the bag Leanne had given her. "Yours are small, and that's always a good sign. How's that hand of yours, all healed up by now I should think. Let's have a look … you can hardly see where the stitches were. Reminds me of when George's dad cut his hand and went to our doctor, lovely woman. He always hated scraping her bottom in the winter. I told him more than once to wear gloves."

Colette giggled. "You mean his boat, *Bethany's,* bottom. Not the doctor's."

"Course I do, whatever made you think that?"

George pecked Colette's cheek. "Bob and Frank are here with their wives, and Tiny's brought a record player for background music 'til the Shades start. I'll try and chat later. Jeanette is watching me like a hawk."

"Poor you, under the thumb already? Where's Leanne?"

"She went to the bar, said she'd see you at the table. Seeing as you're playing later, I reserved the one by the fire doors near the stage."

"Thanks, George. I'll find John, see what the score is."

After stopping to say hello to Bob and Frank, Colette headed to the reserved table.

Leanne was already there. "If looks could kill, they'd be drawing a chalk profile round you by now, Colette!"

"Yeah, I saw her on the other side of the dance-floor. Don't know what George sees in her."

"Don't be catty, sweetheart. That's my job!"

141

"Hi, babe. Wow, you look a knockout. You too, Leanne."

Colette took her bag off the chair next to her. "Take a pew John, when do you want me?"

"Anytime, you know that."

"I mean to play, stupid sod."

Leanne picked up her drink. "Look, if you two are talking shop, I'll go and say hi to Bob and Frank. I've not met their wives."

"Just as well she left, babe. I've some news that's just between us, right?"

Colette grinned. "You want me to sign the official secrets act, John?"

"Silly bugger. You heard Le Page is in the hospital?"

"The grapevine does reach St. Sampson's you know."

"It was Speedy and me. We had a score to settle."

"Can't say I'm sorry. Or surprised knowing you."

"Two birds with one stone, babe!"

Colette looked puzzled. "I don't get it."

"One of the lads who got beaten up at the Spencer Davis concert last year was my cousin Tony, Speedy's brother. He only confirmed who it was when he heard about you on Sark."

"It's a relief for sure. You did him over good and proper I heard."

"Yeah, we did. The heat will be on for a bit, but contacts tell me the investigation is just cursory. The pigs are unofficially pleased Le Page got it. I'll be away for a while anyway."

Colette raised her eyebrows. "Odd time for a holiday?"

"A few weeks back, we did a demo tape for a major label. They sent a scout over to listen to us. We've signed a contract to support Don Vincent on his UK tour starting next weekend. If all goes well, we'll get some studio time in the new year. Not exactly the big time but a foot in the door."

"I'm impressed, I know Leanne will be over the moon. Last time we were here, she said you should be a star. If you need any original songs, I've got a notepad full of them."

"Didn't know you wrote lyrics, babe."

"The tunes are in my head. I should buy a guitar and reel to reel."

"Cool. Maybe we can get together when I get back. I'm looking out for a studio recorder, you can have mine if I find one. I'll call you on early in the second set, just three or four numbers. I don't want to spoil your evening." He glanced towards the stage. "Lads are getting ready to play, I'd better go. What do you want as your first song?"

Colette thought for a moment. "A Dusty Springfield number, we can figure out the arrangement when you have a break."

"Special to you is it?"

"Yeah, it is, John." She smiled. "George's girlfriend will hate it!"

*

"I told you, Jeanette, I'll sit down when all the guests have arrived."

"Why can't I stay here greeting people with you?"

"Because it's mum's party. You'd want to be the centre of

143

attraction."

"It's your party, too, George."

"I know, but fifty is more important than nineteen."

"I saw you talking to that Colette, or whatever her real name is. I don't know why you had to invite her."

"I didn't invite her, mum did. And anyway, she's my boss."

"Who's that tart with her, another one of your weird friends?"

"Leanne's not a tart, and she's not weird. She owns the company I work for. She's paying for all this."

"She looks like a tart to me. Why don't you go back to your old boatyard? I don't like you working at that place."

"Go and sit down with your friends."

"You haven't even said how nice I look. I bought this mini-skirt especially for your party."

"Your skirt is nice Jeanette, even if it doesn't cover much. But why on earth did you have your hair bleached?"

"I thought you liked blondes!"

"… Just go and sit down."

"I'm going now, but remember one thing, George. You're with me tonight. Don't even think about dancing with Colette."

He was trying to work out how to sneak round to join Colette's table when his mum waylaid him. "What did she want, son?"

"She was moaning about Colette again."

"Just like your cousin Jerry, always complaining."

"She complains because you and her mother insist on calling her

Jerry when her name is Geraldine."

"We've always called her that, so she ought to be used to it by now. Why was your girlfriend moaning about Colette? She's lovely. You should get back together with her."

"I can't, mum."

"Why not, son?"

"I just can't, that's all."

"Well, I like her. She's like you, George. She's different."

*

John kissed Colette, and to rapturous applause, she stepped down from the stage and returned to her seat.

"That was great, sweetheart. I loved the Dusty Springfield song."

"Yeah, I saw you singing along."

"I thought you'd done it to piss off Jeanette, then George walked out. I wonder what that was all about."

"Dunno, but I think we're about to find out. He's coming over."

Leanne turned to look. "I'm outta here, again. Good luck."

"Sit down, George. If you dare, that is. Did you apply for a leave of absence?"

"She's getting to me. She watches my every move."

"It's jealousy. I felt it about you once, so I know how it feels."

"You're kidding! When was that?"

"At the Royal, that first night we all went out together. You were talking to Jeanette by the door."

"I'm a bloody fool! She's not half the woman you are, Colette."

"You've been drinking, George. You'll regret saying that tomorrow at work."

"Sure, I've had a few. But it doesn't stop me from feeling bad about you."

"Why did you walk out during my Dusty Springfield song?"

"You were looking in my direction as if you were singing it just for me."

"I was singing it for you. I was telling you something that I can't say to your face."

His hair fell forward. "The title line … You don't have to say you love me. That did it for me, Colette. I realised how it could have been."

She touched his hand. "I didn't hear what you said."

He looked up. "You don't have to say you love me."

"Come on, the band's playing a slow number." She gripped his hand a little tighter. "Let's dance, I'm feeling romantic."

"I can't. She'd go berserk."

She let go of his hand. "Go back to her, George! Let's pretend we never had this conversation."

He looked across to where Jeanette was sitting, then back to Colette. "Why do I feel like this about you?"

She grinned. "Because I'm gorgeous?"

"Yeah, that'd be it." He got up to leave. "I'd better get back to the wicked witch."

*

"You just had to go and talk to her didn't you, George. I don't like her. You know that."

"She's a guest, I've spoken to everyone here."

"I don't even know why I'm calling her 'her.' She's not even a proper woman."

"That's a nasty thing to say, Jeanette."

"No dress sense either. No-one wears black nowadays, and showing her legs off like that is disgusting."

"Your mini-skirt is shorter than her dress."

"I know, but I'm a woman, and she's not!"

"You already said that."

"But it's true, George. They should lock people like that away. She's mental!"

"Settle down. You're getting angry for no reason."

"Just look at her! She's dancing with the singer."

"She can dance with whoever she wants. It's nothing to do with you."

"It is when I have to look at what they're doing. It makes me sick."

He turned to see Colette and John kissing passionately on the dancefloor. "Other couples are kissing, too. What's the problem?"

"She's doing it on purpose to get at me and make you jealous, George. Can't you see that?"

He stood up. "I can't put up with this, Jeanette. You're fucking paranoid!"

While John danced with Colette, Speedy and Tiny continued with a slow Beatles medley.

"Just like old times, babe. We'd best stop snogging. I don't want to hack George off, he's a good guy."

"He's too good for Jeanette."

"Make a play for him then. I know you can do it."

"You don't understand, John. He has to want me for what I am. I can't give him what she can."

"I'm needed back on stage, babe. If I don't see you before we leave on Friday, I'll be in touch when we get back."

One last lingering kiss with John, and Colette returned to her table. "I had to say goodbye to him, Leanne. The Shades are leaving for the mainland next weekend."

"Yeah, Danny told me in the break. Did you see George walk out again?"

"I didn't dance with John to annoy him."

"I don't think it's you who pissed him off, sweetheart. Jeanette looked furious about something."

"We'll find out soon enough; she's heading our way!"

"I'm staying put this time. Looks like she's on the warpath."

Seething with rage, Jeanette stopped just short of Colette. "Leave George alone. He's my boyfriend, not yours. And cover yourself up." She turned to Leanne. "Both of you. This is his birthday party, not a nightclub."

Colette tried hard to keep a straight face, but Leanne was fired up. "You've come over here looking like a cheap slut with your bleached hair, showing your fat arse off to anyone not quick enough to look away, and you've got the fucking nerve to tell us to cover up, Jeanette? You're annoyed because your boyfriend sat here talking to Colette who's done nothing to you. If you were at all grown up, you'd know this isn't the fucking Soviet Union. George can speak to whoever he likes!"

"Not while he's with me he can't, and especially not with her." She turned back to Colette. "You think you're so clever! Singing your pathetic songs on stage, and sticking your tongue down John Norman's throat on the dance-floor. It's sickening. If you want to be a woman, start acting like one!" She picked up Colette's drink, threw it over her, and stormed off.

Colette shot to her feet. "The bitch, I'm fucking soaked!"

Leanne caught hold of her arm. "Hey, just put it down to experience, sweetheart. Something to tell your grandkids about, eh?"

Colette flinched. Leanne's words had hit a nerve. "You know damned well that's never likely to happen."

Chapter 12 - A Gibson Les Paul

The Monday after George's birthday party was a big day for the boatyard at St. Sampson's. Colette had planned the launch of the Seabourne boat with as much detail as she had the disastrous launch of *St. Terethe*. However, this time James was not present, and Graham Le Page was in hospital recovering from a beating.

The launch went without a hitch. But the events of the night before had created a rift between her and George.

Richard Seabourne was not only very wealthy but was generous, too. He'd employed caterers to provide a hot buffet lunch for his friends and the boatyard staff before the launch, and made sure there was ample champagne available as his boat was lowered down the slipway. He'd also arranged a private celebration at the English and Guernsey Arms after a brief trip around the harbour along with a select few friends.

When Colette and George had helped the last passenger to disembark at the quay, it fell to them to do the final checks before joining the celebration. It was the perfect opportunity for Colette to clear the air.

After a friendly call on the VHF set to the Harbour Master, George turned off the radio and threw the isolation switch. "That's it then. All good this time, Colette."

"It's a relief to have her tied up safe and sound. But before we enjoy Mr Seabourne's hospitality, let's sit down in the cabin for a bit, eh? There's beer in the fridge, and we need to talk."

George opened two canned lagers and set them on the pedestal table. "It's about last night, isn't it? I wasn't drunk, you know. Your song told me more than I could ever guess."

Colette picked up a can. "We can talk about that if you want, but I was thinking about Jeanette's vindictiveness."

"She was out of order. She won't apologise, so I'm doing it for her. If your dress needs cleaning, I'll willingly pay for it."

"Don't be a prat, George. You know damned well it's not about the dress. It's about you! You're not the same person as you were. She's got you hooked."

"You sound like my mum. She can't stand Jeanette either."

"I didn't say I don't like her. I do think she's a bit juvenile, though. You've lived on the island all your life. You must have seen how the girls don't have any ambitions other than to find a man and get married? They're nest builders. I'm an outsider, and I can see it a mile off."

"You've hit the nail with that one. Jeanette's been talking engagement for weeks and pestering me to sell *Bethany.*"

"No, bloody no! Whatever happens, don't do that. It would break your mum's heart, and yours. Mine, too, come to that. If you need money, I've got a bit saved, it's yours."

"I don't have much, and sometimes it's a struggle, but I get by. I help mum out when I can, and she's very frugal, we manage."

"I love your mum to bits! She's the nicest person I've met on Guernsey."

151

"Some people think she's muddleheaded. But mum's the most perceptive person you could wish to meet. You know what she said to me at the party?"

"Go on."

"She said you're different, and I'm different, too. I can't figure out that last bit."

"I can … but you've got to work it out for yourself."

"Mum wants me to get back together with you, and after your song last night I think she may be right."

"Only you can make up your mind, George. All I can say is I meant what I said. You don't have to say you love me."

"That line again. I can't say it yet. Maybe when I've figured myself out, I might be able to … but I do feel it."

Colette stood up. "Feeling it is fine with me. Let's go get that drink with Mr Seabourne, eh?"

"Good plan, boss. It's a celebration for me too. Last night, after you left, I told the wicked witch to find herself another fool. I'm a free man again!"

*

"Dinner's almost ready, sweetheart. Throw another log on the stove, and I'll set the table."

Colette was happy that Leanne had taken on the role of homemaker and provider. After the attempted rape in September, she needed close friendship more than intimacy.

Leanne placed a beef casserole and dipping bread on the table.

152

"You had a letter from home today, and you've been quiet ever since."

"They want me to go back for the holidays. I've been thinking about it."

"Only two weeks to Christmas Day come Monday. Flights will be all booked up if you don't make your mind up soon."

"I have made my mind up. I can't revert to being Colin for the week. It'd be like living a lie. What about you?"

Leanne dipped a chunk of bread and hesitated. "Well, if you're sure you're staying here, I'll book flights and a hire car for next weekend, take presents to the twins, then spend Christmas and New Year with my mother in Cumberland. I'll call you when I can, but I know the boatyard will be in good hands while I'm away."

*

John kept his word about the reel to reel recorder he'd mentioned before the Shades went on tour. A brief phone call to say he was coming over and he appeared at the apartment twenty minutes later.

While he lugged the bulky machine up the stairs, Colette held the door open for him. "Thanks, John. I can get all my songs down on tape now. Are you sure you won't need it?"

"Keep it as long as you want, babe. I got a deal on a Sony studio machine from a sound guy at the Ipswich Gaumont."

"My hometown, I wish I could've been there. How was the tour?"

"On the road for twenty-eight days takes it out of you, and backing an ageing Doo-Wop singer trying to be hip was kind of

153

quirky. But we all had a laugh, and the chicks were cool."

Colette grinned. "I'm sure they were, John. Just remember what I said on the phone. This session is strictly music, alright?"

"I get it, babe, and I'm sorry I got carried away at George's party."

"No need to apologise. I was using you to piss off Jeanette."

"And make George jealous?"

She paused. "Yeah, that too, and I think it worked."

John took a cigarette from a pack on the coffee table. "I shouldn't tell you this, but he came to see me when I got back. One mixed up kid you have there. You need to sort him out, *really* sort him out, if you know what I mean."

"His mum invited me to Christmas dinner, and he's coming here on Boxing Day." Her eyes twinkled. "Maybe I'll do it then, eh?" John had also brought an acoustic guitar. She picked it up. "Right, down to business. Thanks for bringing this. I didn't get around to buying one yet."

John tapped the side of his nose. "Don't buy a guitar! Can't say more than that, sorry."

Colette gave him a sideways look, then handed over her songwriting notepad. "Scan through that and say when you see one you like. I've noted the chord sequence, tempo and key at the top of each page. That'll give you an idea of genre."

For over an hour Colette played each one that he called out. She didn't need to look at her notepad. Her memory for song lyrics and music was exceptional.

John liked them all, then turned back to one he'd skipped over earlier. "You didn't get around to noting the chords and tempo, no title either."

"That one's been bugging me. The lyrics came easy, but I've got this weird notion of tempo. A strong off-beat at one-twenty-eight. Simple bass in the verse, but walking in the chorus." She played a bass riff on the low E and A strings to demonstrate. "I'll play the rhythm part, but a single guitar won't cut it. You'll have to imagine the bass and drums working together really tight."

"Hold it there, babe. I can vocalise the bass sounds, but I need a drum kit." John went through to the kitchen and rummaged in cupboards and drawers. Returning with a wooden chopping board and a Tupperware container, he placed them on the coffee table. Holding a large pair of chopsticks, he was ready. "All set! Now let's see what we can do with that number."

With John's accompaniment on the makeshift drums and bass vocals, Colette played it through. "What do you think?"

"It's got potential. Needs some harmonies and something to make it unique, though."

"It's the band that needs to be unique, John."

"A rock band is a rock band, babe. Three guitars and a drummer."

Colette sat forward. It was time to tell him of an idea she'd been thinking about for a while. "Your line-up is fine. But smart casual is bland, and it's been overdone. Read the first part again. It'll show what I mean without me explaining."

Nineteen. They say I look just like a glamour girl.

My dream. I'm happy in my glamour world.

(four-bar break)

My way. A revolution of a different kind.

I say. Together we will blow their minds.

"Good lyrics for you, babe. We'd have to change the 'glamour girl' bit for us though."

"No way. That's the point of the song. If you read on, you'll see it's the story of a macho guy who wants to be glamorous in a feminine way. The Stones did leather jackets and jeans, and The Beatles are currently pushing the boundary with colourful uniforms. When I was Colin, Leanne noticed me wearing a pink ribbon. It's a long story. I made a joke that all the lads will be wearing their hair like that one day, so I wrote that song."

"I get it … but you said the band needs to be unique?"

She took the notepad, turned to the second from last page and held up a coloured ink drawing of a bearded guitarist wearing a glittery blouse, pink and blue knee boots with thick high heels, and gold satin pantaloons. "Flower Power won't last forever, John. Don't follow the trend. Lead it! You need to be outrageous to get noticed."

"Bloody hell, that's me! I didn't know you were an artist. I think you've got something. Tiny would go for it, and don't ask me how I know, but there's no chance of Speedy and Danny doing that."

She handed John her notepad. "Well, it's just an idea. I did Tiny

156

as well, just his face."

John stared for several seconds. "Wow, that is amazing! The eyeshadow is freaky, and that shooting star design on one cheek is striking. Where did you get the inspiration?"

"Leanne told me once that I needed something weird for a rhyme I was looking for. That got me thinking. If a song can be weird, why not the band, too? You can take those drawings to show the others if you want."

John set up a microphone on the coffee table. "We'll record that one, and I'll play it to the boys. If they like it, I'll make a demo tape and send it to the record company. Let's hope the producer has the same vision as you, babe."

*

In the apartment, Colette didn't usually make too much effort to feminise, especially with Leanne being away. But today was special. George was arriving to spend Boxing Day with her. She'd got up early, soaked in scented foam, selected the shortest mini-dress in her wardrobe, taken great care of her makeup and hair, and splashed on enough Chanel No 5 to capture Robert Vaughn—her favourite actor—let alone George Bisson. She'd just put the vegetables on to steam when a vehicle pulled into the courtyard; that old Ford Prefect van had a sound all of its own.

George came into the kitchen and kissed her a little longer than was necessary for a greeting. This was promising, she thought.

"Mmm, that smells delicious, Colette."

"The dinner or my man trap perfume?"

"Both, and you look gorgeous, too."

"You're not so bad yourself, Mr Bisson. Can't say I've ever seen you wear a suit before, though. Are you going somewhere special after dinner, or is that for me?"

He grimaced. "Mum's idea. You made the effort yesterday at our house, so she insisted I wear it. Can I take the tie off? It's bloody killing me."

"Be my guest. Anything else you want to dispense with? Jacket, or trousers perhaps?"

George flushed scarlet. "Uh, just the jacket, I think. Um, changing the subject, thanks again for the marine radio for *Bethany*. It was a very generous gift. I'll install it before she goes back in the water in the spring. Your present is in the van. I'll give it to you after dinner if that's ok."

"I can't wait." She opened the fridge. "Here's a beer, go and check the stove for me and make yourself comfortable. We eat in ten minutes."

Colette was careful not to come on to George too much during the meal. She didn't want to embarrass him more than she had already. Sexual puns about roast beef and steamed vegetables were limited, and thick gravy wasn't at all erotic as far as she knew.

She was intrigued by the gift George had brought for her. John's cryptic mention had given her a clue, but she was impatient to find out. Maybe an innuendo was needed to hurry him up. "That's the washing up done, and thanks for helping. Don't you have something for me? Is it big?"

"It's down in the van. Do you want me to get it up for you now? Shit, what have I just said?"

She giggled. "You know what my reply should be, but just go and fetch it, eh?"

She thought about watching from the balcony, but that would spoil his surprise. His returning footsteps on the stairway were clumsy and laboured. At last, he struggled into the living room and set down a big bulky square object with a handle that poked out of the Christmas wrapping paper, and a long, flat, rectangular object, also beautifully wrapped. Kneeling on the floor, she read the gift tags.

The bulky one said: *'To my best friend, with so much love, Leanne xx'*

The long one said: *'à une fille très spéciale, Noël 1967, je t'aime, gros bisous, George.'*

Brushing away a tear, she looked up. "You've been in collusion with Leanne! I can't read French, what does yours say?"

"We knew what you wanted, so I went to see John. There's a card from me inside the long one. I wrote it in English."

She carefully unwrapped George's gift revealing a black guitar case. No big surprise there, but she wasn't prepared for what was inside. "It's a fucking Gibson, oops. It's a Gibson Les Paul, no way. I can't believe it."

"You're pleased then?"

"Pleased? I'm bloody ecstatic! You do know you've bought me the very best guitar in the whole wide world, don't you?"

"Yeah, that's what John said."

It suddenly kicked in how much this instrument would have cost. "Take it back George! You can't afford to buy this for me."

"It's only second-hand, but John said it was a good one."

"I don't care, even second-hand, it will still have been bloody expensive."

George sounded agitated. "I don't know anything about guitars. John told me he'd acquired it in a job lot and was happy to let it go at a low price. I wouldn't have bought it otherwise."

So, John was in on this too. She should be grateful and figure it out later. "Oh, I'm sorry. I'm so thrilled to have it, thank you."

"Open your present from Leanne."

After unwrapping the guitar, she knew what the bulky gift might be. But again, she was surprised. "Wow, it's a Vox AC30, just wow. A perfect combination amplifier to go with the Gibson, and don't tell me. John said that!"

George laughed. "How did you guess?"

"I've got to try them, I've just got to." She picked up the guitar, and her heart sank; his card was underneath. "I'm sorry, George. I was so excited about the presents I forgot about this."

He pretended nonchalance. "Don't worry, it's nothing really. Just me being silly."

She gave him a sheepish look, then withdrew the card from a pink envelope. *'To A Very Special Friend'* was written above a seasonal design on the front. She looked inside and read his words several times.

He held out his hands to help her stand up. "I told you, I can't say it yet. But I can write it."

She was close to tears. "How do I say, I love you, too?"

He touched her cheek and thumbed away a wet streak of mascara. "You just did."

"In French I mean. I may have to say it often."

"It's ... moi aussi, je t'aime."

She took a deep breath and spoke slowly, "moi - aussi - je t'aime." She remembered something else on the gift tag. "But there was more. Gros bis something."

"I'd rather show you what gros bisous means, Colette." He took her in his arms and kissed her passionately. "Now go play with your new toys."

John had thought of everything. Tucked inside the back of the amplifier she found a good quality guitar cable, a tuner, spare set of strings, and a packet of assorted picks. For well over an hour, she played every song that George asked for and a few of her own compositions. By late afternoon, sore fingertips told her it was time to stop. "I'll brew some coffee, and we'll have a slice of the Christmas cake your mum insisted I bring home."

He stretched and smiled. "I could get used to this."

161

Returning with a tray, she couldn't help noticing that he looked thoughtful. "Cheer up. It might never happen."

He took the offered mug. "Yeah, that's what I'm afraid of, Colette, and I wouldn't know what to do if it did."

She'd intended to snuggle next to him on the sofa. But because he sounded as if he wanted to talk, she chose the armchair instead. "Bloody hell, are we getting deep, or what?"

His long black hair fell forward. "I told you I went to see John."

This was no time to be frivolous, she spoke softly. "For the guitar, yes?"

"He's a cool guy. We had a long talk about you."

"Just about me?"

"About me, too. Well, mostly about me, really."

She didn't quite know where this was leading. "You want to tell me about it, pet?"

Surprised, he looked up. "You've never called me 'pet' before."

"You've never told me you love me before."

He smiled. "I didn't actually say it."

"Yeah, that's true. So, what did wise old John Norman tell you? Did he read your palm, or feel your bumps?"

"Just leave my bumps out of this," he quipped, then became serious again. "I was worried that I might be bisexual."

"Nothing wrong with that … are you?"

"The thought of intimacy with a man turns me off. I couldn't do that."

162

"So, how do you see me?"

"To me, Colette, you are a woman and a very beautiful one at that. You don't know how much sleep I've lost trying to figure out how it could be between us. I know we'd be great as partners, but it's the other thing I can't get my head around."

"Sex, you mean?"

"Yeah, but there's one thing I just couldn't do."

"Anal sex?"

"See, I can't even bring myself to say it."

"I couldn't do that either, pet. So you're not alone."

He relaxed back on the sofa. "That's a relief, but what's left?"

She thought for a moment. "I know this is not going to sound romantic, but how about some ground rules, so we know where we stand with each other? I'll go first if you like."

"I can live with that, Colette. Go on."

"There's only two for me. One I just said I couldn't do, and the other is—she pointed downwards—don't ever attempt to touch me 'there.' Now, what are yours?"

He looked relieved. "Apart from agreeing to your two I don't have any, and it's a huge weight off my mind."

She gave him a wicked look. "Just one more thing then."

Knowing what was coming, he cringed. "Um, what's that?"

"We need to see if it works for us, eh, pet?"

He made an awkward face. "Please don't think I'm avoiding it, Colette, but I need a bit of thinking time. I'm sorry."

*

Because Christmas Day was Monday, Leanne had given her workers the remainder of the week off as a bonus and a thank you for their support.

Colette had agreed to give George the thinking time he needed. This suited her because she was keen to record her songs, and if he was around, she wasn't sure she'd get much done. He'd called to say that the Shades were playing a New Year's Eve gig at The Fermain Tavern and he'd love to take her.

It turned out to be fun to relax and enjoy the gig from the audience. George was at the bar when the band announced a break. John came over to the table where Colette was sitting. "Where were you, babe? I thought you'd be here at eight to set up with that new guitar of yours."

She gave him a mock slap. "Whatever are you on? Tonight's for George and me. The Gibson's fab, though. It's perfect with the AC30. You'll have to tell me the real story of it sometime."

He winked at her. "Sorry, babe. I'm sworn to secrecy. Did you sort your man out?"

She smiled ruefully. "Getting there, John, getting there."

John nodded. "Listen, the boys have a surprise for you, so pay attention first number after the break, ok? Must dash, not much time." He hurried off leaving Colette bewildered.

George returned to find her still looking puzzled. "I saw you talking to John. Everything alright?"

"I'm not sure. I have a sneaky feeling something's going on that certain people are keeping from me. Are you part of this Mr Bisson?"

"Um … am I allowed to lie if it's for a good cause?"

"No! Spill the beans or I'll squeeze you where it hurts most!"

"All I can say is that John called and asked me to make sure you were here before ten-thirty. Other than that, I'm in the dark as much as you!"

A few minutes later, there were gasps from the back of the room, and people at the other tables were standing up to see what was going on. From where Colette and George were sitting it was impossible to know the cause, but several camera flashes indicated that it was something worth seeing.

When the disturbance reached the stage, Colette's eyes opened wide with disbelief. "That's exactly like my drawing! John's got it spot-on, right down to the pink and blue boots."

George's jaw dropped. "I've never seen anything like it!"

"And Tiny's make-up is perfect, even the shooting star on his cheek."

"It's a New Year stunt, Colette. Can't be anything else."

She couldn't take her eyes off John and Tiny, then she noticed the others. "It's their new look. I invented it. Even Speedy and Danny have dressed the same way."

George wrenched his eyes away. "Well, it's certainly caused a storm. I know I shouldn't say this, but Tiny is beautiful, no other word for it."

The revellers went quiet as John stepped up to the microphone. "Thanks, everyone. I hope you all like our new image. Many of you will know Colette who designed this new look, but that's not all. She wrote a song for us, and today we heard that we'll be recording it as our debut single. You all wanna hear it?"

The crowd erupted, and Colette was gobsmacked. "I can't believe this. I'm so happy for John and the boys."

Throughout the song, George gripped her hand, and when it was over, he kissed her. "I'm very proud of you. You believed in yourself. I admire you for that." He picked up her empty glass. "I'll get you another drink, this calls for a celebration."

She took it from him. "No! This is your night, too. It's gone eleven, and I know there's something you want me to see."

George drove with a satisfied grin, the dim headlights of his old Ford Prefect van barely lighting up the road ahead. "You'll know where we're heading when we reach the next bend."

She leaned forward, anxious to know where this mystery ride was leading. "The airport! Bloody hell George. I hope it's the mainland, I don't have my passport with me."

He laughed. "I'm not taking you anywhere exotic, but somewhere on Guernsey that is special for me, and I hope will be special for you, too."

She opened the glove compartment and checked her watch by its faint light. "Twenty to midnight. You'll have to stop soon so I can kiss you Happy New Year."

"Another five minutes and we'll be there."

The van veered slightly caught by the wind as he made a right turn at a T junction. "Where are we now, George?"

"That's L'Erée Headland up ahead. I've been coming here since I was a child. The beach on your side was one of my dad's favourite places."

"You'll have to bring me here in daylight. I can't see a thing."

He turned left off the main road and into a small deserted parking area. "This is it, Colette. Only a few yards to walk and we'll be there."

"Just as well I brought a warm coat. It looks like a bloody tempest out there."

He reached over to the rear of the van and grabbed two blankets. "These will keep us snug." He took a small flashlight from the dashboard and checked his watch. "Ten minutes to go. Come on. You don't want to miss it."

Colette followed him along a rough footpath to a rocky shore, a feat she was surprised to accomplish in heels. George laid one blanket on the coarse grass and motioned Colette to sit down. Sitting beside her, he wrapped the other blanket around their shoulders.

She gripped a corner to stop it blowing away. "What are we waiting for?"

"Listen, do you hear that?"

She had to shout. "George! I can hardly hear what you're saying, let alone anything else. The wind is fierce, and the sea is so rough, it might as well be a bloody hurricane."

He leaned in close to her. "That's the point!"

"What?"

"That's the whole point, Colette." He waited for a crashing wave to subside. "Other than the force of nature there's nothing but you and me. Doesn't that make you feel something?"

She turned to him, barely making out his boyish grin. "Yeah, it's like we're the only two people on the planet! It's magical. Now I know why you brought me here. It's this place isn't it?"

Another breaker hit the shore, its spray wetting their faces. George flicked on the flashlight and held it to Colette's wrist. "One minute to go!" he shouted.

A strong gust of wind tore the blanket from her grasp. She tried to retrieve it, but it was gone. With her hair flying about wildly, she glanced over her left shoulder. "Look, over there in the distance. It must be midnight."

"Someone's celebrating with fireworks in Pleinmont."

Another wave swept spray over them. He drew her close and kissed her. "Happy nineteen-sixty-eight, Colette."

She responded passionately. "Happy New Year, George. Shouldn't we make a resolution or something?"

"Resolutions are for breaking. I'd rather take life as it comes."

"There's something in that, I guess." She leaned forward and pointed. "I'm sure I saw a light out there. It looked too close to be a ship."

"It's Lihou island, that's where the magic comes from. There's just one house and a ruined priory hundreds of years old. In the summer the sunsets over Lihou are spectacular."

"I want to share that with you." She wiped spray from her eyes. "Shouldn't we be getting back to the van?"

"Poor you, your hair's a mess, you're soaked, and you're cold." He eased her back onto the grass. "But look up for a moment, there's a break in the cloud. Have you ever seen stars so bright?"

"I can almost reach out and touch them. It's like the universe is at my fingertips."

"Dad always said if you want something badly enough, and reach out far enough, nothing is impossible." He lay down beside her and held her hair away from her face. "I love you so very much, Colette."

A tear mingled with the spray on her cheek. "You said it! You said you love me. I'm so happy. Je t'aime très fort ... I looked that up."

He laughed. "Come on little miss clever clogs. It's time I took you home."

"Bacon and eggs or cereal?"

"Eh?"

"For your breakfast in bed, pet."

He looked puzzled for a moment, then the penny dropped. "Um, ask me again in the morning. There might be something else you can

169

do for me!"

*

Colette removed the key, pulled hard on the workshop door to make sure it was secure, then got into the passenger seat of George's van. "Don't know about you, but I'm bushed."

"Yeah, the first day back to work is always the hardest."

She rested her hand on his thigh. "You'll miss sleeping with me tonight."

He gave her a sideways glance. "Have we slept? I didn't notice."

She smiled. "I think we did, just for an hour or two." Her hand moved to his crotch. "You enjoyed your breakfasts though."

"Colette!" he yelled. "For fuck's sake, not while I'm driving ... please."

She withdrew and pretended to sulk. "Spoilsport, it was only my hand. It could have been my tongue! You've not complained about that for the last two days."

He smiled. "That was a first for me. I never knew such pleasure existed."

She licked her lips provocatively. "Leanne will be back in the apartment by now, but we can stop on the way home if you like?"

"Um, no. After two nights with you, I need to get my strength back."

She waved him off, crossed the courtyard, and climbed the stairs. Opening the apartment door, the aroma of something spicy cooking made her mouth water.

Leanne called from her bedroom. "I'm unpacking, be right out."

"OK, I'll make coffee."

Leanne came into the kitchen and hugged her. "Did you miss me?"

"Yeah, course I did. Thanks for your fab gift. I'm sorry the scarf I bought you wasn't as expensive. Good trip back?"

"Long queue for a taxi at the airport. If John hadn't been dropping someone off, I'd still be waiting. He told me about the band and your song. I'm so pleased for you. You've not been too lonely while I was away, I hope."

Colette smiled to herself and slid Leanne's Fab Four mug along the countertop. "George stayed over a couple of nights."

Leanne said nothing. Turning to the hob, she lifted a lid and stirred.

"I'm sorry, Leanne, but I can't lie about it."

"Did you have sex?"

Colette knew this was an unreasonable question, but Leanne deserved to know. "Yes, sort of. As much as I was comfortable doing. He didn't complain."

Leanne turned, her eyes glistening. "I need a hug. I know I've lost you, but I can handle it. Just don't shut me out of your life. You're all I've got now."

"I don't understand."

"No, of course you don't. There are some things an old married woman has to keep from even her best friend. Dinner will be another half hour. Let's go into the living room, and I'll tell you about it."

Colette put their mugs on the coffee table and sat in the armchair opposite Leanne. "I thought you were just taking presents for the twins, what happened?"

"It all started the first week in October. The bank called me to say they'd bounced a company cheque."

"Was that the day you had to go out urgently?"

"It was. Anyway, the short version is that James had been milking the company account. He'd taken thousands."

"Bloody hell! What did you do?"

"I went straight to my lawyer. I couldn't have James' name taken off the boatyard bank account because it was in both our names, so he advised me to open another account and change the company details at the States office. Richard Seabourne was brilliant. He understood my predicament and stopped a cheque he'd sent for his boat. He gave me another one that I deposited in the new account. With that and a large sum that I put in, the yard stayed solvent."

"I was shitty to you around that time. I'm sorry."

"It was too soon after what James did to you, sweetheart. I didn't want to worry you."

"So, how does that tie in with your visit?"

"I did spend Christmas with my mother, but I spent the rest of the time in a Kinross hotel. James was in a right state. He wanted to come back here and carry on as if nothing's happened."

"No way! What did you say?"

"It was my money that he started the boatyard with. I was the sole stakeholder, so I threatened a lawsuit for fraud. I told him I'd drop it if he signed legal ownership of the yard over to me and consent to a divorce."

"Divorce! That sounds so final. Did he agree?"

"He was cornered. His only choice was prison or pauper."

"But he owns the house, doesn't he?"

"He might have given that impression, but the house is mine. Because of a prenuptial agreement, he can't touch it, so we're safe."

"And the twins?"

Leanne stared at Colette for a few seconds then looked away, her eyes welling.

Colette rushed to hold her close. "I'm so sorry, Leanne…"

"It's alright, sweetheart. Not your fault. On the afternoon of New Year's Eve, they both told me they wanted to stay with their father and Liz fucking Previn. They even called her 'Mum' in front of me. Walking away was the hardest thing I've ever had to do."

"I don't know what to say, that's a terrible thing to…"

"I went to a pharmacy and bought three packs of paracetamol, ninety-six tablets in all. After buying a bottle of vodka from an off-licence, I went back to the hotel. Then just before midnight, I opened all the packets, and you know what?"

"No, go on."

"I was so choked up I couldn't swallow any!"

"So that's why you didn't take them?"

"Oh no, but I couldn't stop laughing at my stupidity, I'd started on the bloody vodka by then. I decided to dissolve the tablets in a tumbler of water, it'd taste awful but hey, who cares when you're dead? I knew that ninety-six paracetamol pills would take a long time to become liquid, so I started crushing them with the back of a teaspoon. It was tedious work, but it gave me time to think about all the people who rely on me, especially you, sweetheart. Who would look after you if I wasn't here to do it?"

Chapter 13 - Mistress Georgina

While George retrieved a stepladder from the back of his van, Colette walked over to the model yacht pond. She remembered her first nervous outing back in August last year. It was only six months ago, but so much had happened in her short existence that it seemed much longer.

She turned to face the boatyard where George used to work. Even though it was cold this early February morning, the big doors were open and the noise of a bandsaw somehow complimented an intermittent rat-tat-tat of someone riveting; familiar sounds she knew well. Wearing his old paint-stained khaki jacket, George was in the doorway talking to an older man. He was probably catching up with an ex-workmate, yet their conversation looked serious.

The van was parked next to *Bethany* to the side of the boatyard. She could at least make herself useful until George joined her. Climbing the stepladder, she unfastened the canvas cover and folded it back. Stepping into the cockpit, she unhooked the remainder of the eyelets and rolled the cover towards the stern.

Across St. Peter Port harbour a church bell chimed eleven. She imagined Leanne buying fresh fish in the market for their evening meal and shopping on the High Street, wrapped up warm and wearing sensible shoes to avoid slipping on frosty cobbles; alone this Saturday as she had been for weeks now.

The stepladder creaked, and George's head appeared above the gunwale, his long black hair tied back in a ponytail and a grubby knitted hat pulled down over his ears. He hefted a tool bag over the coaming and climbed aboard looking guilty. "Why can't she just leave me alone?"

Her heart sank. Only one person would cause him to say that. "Who … Jeanette?"

"The very same. That was her uncle Peter. I was his 'lad' when I first came to work here. He keeps an eye on *Bethany* for me."

"So, what's she done now?"

"Uh, nothing I can't deal with."

"You want to tell me about it, pet?"

"No!"

She was hurt. George never snapped at her. "Fine! Let's get on with the job then. Go and fetch the marine radio from the van and pass the flask up. I need a hot drink." She took a test meter and hydrometer from his tool bag. "While you're doing that I'll check the battery voltage and levels."

She watched George climb down the ladder and sighed. How did her life get this complicated?

For two hours, they worked in almost total silence, only communicating when necessary to get the job done. She flung down a screwdriver. She'd been looking forward to this morning. Now Jeanette had spoiled everything. And George was keeping something from her. If she didn't lighten up fast, he'd clam up even more.

George made a brief test call to the Harbour Master, then folded the short antenna flat on the cabin top. "That's it, all finished. I'll take you home now."

Colette checked they'd left nothing in the cabin, then turned to face him. "Look, I'm sorry I was in a mood but you snapped at me, and it's unlike you, pet. If there's something you want to keep to yourself that's fine, but secrets make me jumpy."

He slumped down onto a cockpit seat. "Any of that coffee left?"

She poured two plastic cups of warm grey liquid. "Is it something serious?"

He took a sip and made a face. "How can good coffee taste this bad after two hours in a flask?"

"Don't change the subject."

He took a deep breath, exhaling slowly. "It's your birthday on Wednesday."

"Um, yes, we've both got two days off work. I've booked the flights and hotel for our trip to Jersey, just the two of us, remember?"

"How can I forget your twentieth?"

"For fuck's sake, George. We were only talking about it in the van on the way here. And why did you even need to mention Jeanette when you came on board? You knew it would upset me."

"Her uncle said he'd tell you himself if I didn't."

She eyed him across the cockpit and prepared for the worst. She knew this wasn't going to be good news. "Tell me what?"

"Jeanette's in the hospital. She was taken in early this morning. Her mother telephoned Peter at work just before we arrived. It could be serious."

"Did he say what's wrong with her?"

He lit a cigarette, took a long pull, closed his eyes, and shattered their relationship with two words. "Pregnancy complications."

They stared at each other for what seemed like an eternity. At last, she asked the obvious. "Yours?"

"Yeah."

"How far is she gone?"

"Over four months."

"How long have you known?"

"I got a message to go and see her the middle of January. She told me then."

"When were you going to tell me?"

"After your birthday."

"Have you seen her again since she told you?"

He fiddled with his cigarette, nodded, then looked up. "Yeah, most evenings when I'm not with you."

She could have asked him about his lies and excuses for not being with her, but what would that achieve? She felt nothing, not even anger. It was over. "Take me home, George. You'll need to be getting along to see Jeanette."

While George gripped the steering wheel, his stony gaze on the road ahead, Colette thought about their relationship. It had taken months to blossom into something more than special. He'd accepted her difference from other girls. How many men would do that? At five minutes past midnight on the first of January, he'd said he loved her. Now, five weeks later, she didn't know how he felt.

'I can't cry. I can't even bloody well cry over losing the best thing that's ever happened to me.'

George halted the van in the courtyard, engine running. It was obvious he was keen to get away. She knew he was hurting and she wouldn't make it worse. She owed him that at least. "Hey, come on, put one here." She puckered up and pointed to her lips. "We can't part bad friends now can we."

He leaned over and kissed her. "I've let you down, and I can't see a way out of the mess I'm in. But whatever happens, nothing can stop me loving you."

She couldn't listen to this. She stumbled up the apartment steps. George was turning the van. She couldn't look round.

Leanne was busy putting shopping away. "Did you have a good day, sweetheart?" she shouted. "I saw the van pull up. Coffee in two minutes."

Colette hung her coat on a hook in the hallway then went into the kitchen. "Was I like that when I was Colin?"

Leanne looked puzzled. "Like what?"

"Like a lying, cheating, bastard!"

"Ah … George."

"Yeah, I thought I could trust him, but I was wrong. He's a shit."

Plunging the cafetière, Leanne reached for the whisky bottle and poured a generous measure into both mugs. "Come on girl. I lit the stove when I came home. It'll be warmer in the living room."

*

George drove home in a daze. Telling Colette about the baby wasn't easy, and her reaction was unexpected. Other women wouldn't have taken it so calmly, but that's what he liked about her, she wasn't like other women. His love for her was different from the love he'd once felt for the mother of his unborn child. With Colette, he could share the things in life that were important to him. His boat, *Bethany,* and his chosen trade. She understood how a man thinks because … well, just because. His attraction to her wasn't in spite of the fact she was different, but because of it, and that was something he'd struggled with. After loving Colette, the responsibility of being a father and married to Jeanette was not a comforting thought. But her family would expect it.

He reversed his van into the tiny front garden parking space. He could no longer put off facing his mother.

"Guess what, son. I bumped into your boss in the market, lovely piece of fish, local caught, not even a Friday. How was your day with Colette?"

"Not good, mum. We had an argument. Well, more of a long silence really."

"Ups and downs dear. He always saw my way of thinking in the end, your dad. Give her a day or two, then tell her she was right, she'll come round."

"It's not like that, mum. I've done something to hurt her,

180

something I can't do anything about now."

"Nothing's broken that can't be mended, 'cept eggs, you can't unbreak eggs."

"Not this time. I wish it were different, but it's my fault. I've got to live with it."

"Sit down, son. Standing up's not for being serious. Now, what's so bad that keeps you talking in circles?"

"I've been seeing Jeanette."

"I thought you'd given that one the elbow. If your dad were still alive, he'd give you a right ear bashing. No wonder Colette's not talking, poor girl. She's been good to you, son. Whatever made you do a thing like that?"

"Jeanette's in the hospital, ambulance in the early hours."

"Well, you know I don't think much of her. But I wouldn't wish that on any girl. She could lose the baby."

"You knew, mum?"

"Course I did. It's been the main topic down the market these last two Saturdays. Keep away from her. Before you know it, she'll have you on a lead."

"But it's my child she's carrying. I'm responsible."

"Oh, dearie me, and there was me thinking it took two to make a baby. I must be going doolally in my old age. I don't suppose you'll listen to me, son. But if you've any sense at all, you'll make it up with Colette. I'd rather no grandchildren at all than have that Jeanette as a daughter-in-law."

Leanne placed the cafetière on the stove top to keep warm. "Is it about Jeanette's baby?"

Colette stared open-mouthed. "Am I the only dumb idiot who didn't know about it?"

"I only found out this morning. I bumped into George's mum at the market. She's been taken in, hasn't she?"

"Ambulance in the early hours I was told."

Leanne sank into her favourite armchair. "How would you feel if she lost it?"

Colette looked shocked. "That's a terrible thing to say, Leanne."

"Yes, I know. But it'd solve your problem with George."

"No, it wouldn't. It's not just the baby. He's been seeing her for the past three weeks and I never suspected a thing. I must have 'mug' written across my forehead."

"You've booked the trip to Jersey, too."

"Yeah, tell me about it. Happy bloody birthday!"

Leanne looked thoughtful. "What if you took someone else, sweetheart?"

Their eyes met. Colette guessed what Leanne had in mind. "Are you inviting yourself to my birthday treat?"

"A girly day out would do us both good, what do you say?"

Colette forced a grin. "It's two days."

"All the better. I'll ask the lads at the yard to hold the fort."

"And, it's just one hotel room."

"Oh, is that a problem?"

"No, but I've ordered champagne."

Leanne raised her eyebrows. "That will have room service talking."

"And a double bed."

"I'll sleep on the floor if you want."

Colette giggled. "Leanne Cameron, woman of substance and fashion icon sleeping on the floor of a hotel room? I don't think so."

*

Leanne tipped the Bell Boy and waited until he'd closed the door behind him. "Hey, did you get that look from the receptionist?"

"Yeah, she was cute. Secret smiles must be the in thing." Colette peeked in the en-suite and scanned the room. "Hmm, I'd have thought they'd be here before we arrived."

"What exactly are you talking about?"

"I ordered flowers. It's Valentine's day as well as my birthday."

"The works, eh? George doesn't know what he's lost, sweetheart."

"His stupidity and…" A knock on the door stopped her short. She grinned at Leanne. "Come in. We're decent."

When the door opened, an enormous flower arrangement entered the room. "Special delivery for George," it said, then lowered to reveal a surprised looking middle-aged man in a hotel uniform. "Oh, just the two of you?"

Leanne winked at him. "A girly treat for Valentine's."

Colette nodded agreement. "My birthday, too."

He looked at the girls in turn, glanced at the double bed, then read out the card. "To George, with all my love, Colette … have I got the wrong room?"

Leanne pretended to be serious. "This is my girlfriend Colette, and I'm George. It's her pet name for me. I'm sure you'll be discreet."

"Oh, I will, darlings, of course I will. Never let it be said that Gerald can't keep a secret." He placed the flowers on a table teasing one or two stray blooms into place. "I'll see you at the Valentine's Ball tonight, I hope. My Shirley is so looking forward to it, he works in the restaurant."

Before he left, Leanne folded a ten-shilling note and pressed it into his hand. "We wouldn't miss it for the world."

Leanne picked up her bag. "Come on, girl. If we're going to a Ball tonight, we'd best hit the fashion stores. Gerald has given me an idea!"

Even on a mid-February afternoon, shopping in St. Helier was exciting, especially when looking for something special to wear.

In only the second shop they visited, Colette spotted the very thing. A simple but chic, close-fitting, ankle-length dress in a rich ruby colour.

"Wow, that's gorgeous, sweetheart. I can just see you in it, a silver clutch bag and shoes, and a studded collar."

Collette made a face. "Studded collar?"

"Trust me. A black leather studded collar is exactly what that dress needs. There's a small shop just around the corner where we can buy one, and don't ask me how I know."

"But look at the tag, it's twenty-five guineas..."

"Bugger the price! I'll buy it for your birthday."

"What about you?"

"I brought a black trouser suit. All I need is to visit a men's shop for a dress shirt and bow tie. If the hotel staff are gossiping, let's give them something to gossip about, eh?"

Colette giggled. "So, George is going to make an appearance after all!"

"Oh no. Tonight I'm going to be your mistress, Madame Georgina!"

After showering, and Leanne doing her hair, Colette applied her makeup and put on the dress and fashionable silver shoes she'd bought. "Can you fasten the collar for me?"

Wearing a white shirt, black bow tie and suit, and her hair slicked back and held in place with a comb, Leanne stood behind Colette buckling the collar under her hair. "You look sensational, sweetheart. I think the ballroom should be suitably full by now. Let's go and make our entrance."

Holding hands with Leanne, Colette stepped out of the elevator. One or two late-arriving tuxedos and pink dresses were heading towards the ballroom, and the muffled sound of a dance band playing *Moonlight Serenade* drifted across the hotel lobby.

The same girl who was at reception when they arrived was on the telephone and Gerald, their friendly room service guy, called them over. He gave Leanne a knowing look then spoke to Colette. "Oh, Mrs Bisson, that frock so suits you, dear. My Shirley will be green with envy."

Luckily, Leanne's grasp hid her ring finger. She'd forgotten in whose name she'd made the hotel booking. "Um, call me Colette, please."

Gerald looked Leanne up and down. "And you love, so handsome." He pointed surreptitiously to the reception girl behind him and whispered. "Hazel will be having sweet dreams about you tonight, that's for sure."

As the muffled music stopped, Hazel replaced the telephone receiver and smiled at Colette. "Happy birthday, Sis." She switched her attention to Leanne. "Have a lovely evening, Sir. You can go in now."

Colette couldn't help smiling as Gerald escorted them to the ballroom. So much for his discretion. But Leanne didn't seem at all surprised.

Having performed on stage several times, Colette was used to the bright lights. But she wasn't prepared for a spotlight to follow her and 'Mistress Georgina' across the vast ballroom to their table while the band played Happy Birthday. Gerald held her chair for her to be seated, and Shirley appeared bearing a bottle of champagne in an ice bucket.

Colette wondered about the VIP treatment. Surely this couldn't be just for her birthday. Then she noticed a copy of a local Channel Islands newspaper propped up against a floral table decoration. She picked it up and looked closer. Over a picture of John's band, a headline read: 'Guernsey band hits UK charts.'

Leanne sat grinning. "I'm sorry I couldn't tell you, sweetheart." She glanced at Gerald. "While you were in the shower, this lovely man came to the room. He'd seen a photo in that newspaper and wanted to know if it was you. It's on the next page. They must have got it from John."

Colette was speechless. She turned the page. Above a mini-skirted guitar-playing photograph of herself on stage, a sub-headline read: 'Talented singer-songwriter responsible for local band's success.'

Gerald shooed Shirley away and put his arm around Colette. "I'll leave you to it, love. The manager says your drinks are on the house tonight. We often get important people staying here, but you're a Guernsey girl, and that's special."

*

Slumping down into the armchair, Leanne kicked off her shoes. "How does it feel being a superstar?"

Eyeing Leanne in the dressing table mirror, Colette paused from removing her makeup. "I still can't believe it. I knew the Shades had recorded my song back in January, and I heard it played on Caroline a couple of times last week, but John's not been in touch."

"He probably didn't want to get your hopes up. What are your plans for the royalties?"

"Won't amount to much, I shouldn't think. I'm no Jackie DeShannon."

Crossing the room, Leanne slid her hands beneath Colette's hair. "You don't need to be, sweetheart. I love you just the way you are."

Reaching up, Colette held Leanne's hands on the studded collar. "Do you want me to keep this on for you in bed?"

"Are you kidding? It's so bloody sexy."

"Do you remember that night I was in a foul mood, and you brought me a hot drink in bed?"

"How can I forget?" She kissed Colette's cheek. "We slept together for a few nights after that. I miss you terribly."

"But I still couldn't do, you know … it."

"It doesn't matter. We did most everything else last time, didn't we?"

Colette smiled. "Yeah, we did. But I feel I let you down."

Leanne's grip tightened on Colette's shoulders. "What are you saying, sweetheart?"

Colette caught Leanne's eye in the mirror. "Well, if my Mistress Georgina ordered me to do it, I would have to comply. Wouldn't I?"

Chapter 14 – Sunset over Lihou

Colette topped-up everyone's glasses. "Thanks, guys, another successful launch."

Bob grinned. "We're getting the hang of it now."

"It's a bit of a worry that we don't have a buyer for this one." Frank pointed to an almost completed cruiser visible through the office window. "Still, it's only March. The first bit of nice weather and she'll sell, mark my words."

Leanne held up her glass. "Well done, and here's to the next one. I know business is slow, but I've ordered another set of mouldings, so there's work for everyone."

The office door opened and George appeared looking flustered. He dumped a sheaf of paperwork on Leanne's desk. "Sorry I'm late for the celebration. The plant hire manager wanted to know how his new tractor performed." He took a glass from Colette. "Driving back past the harbour I noticed one of the fenders skewed. Think we should check it out?"

Colette put down her drink. "Yeah, sure. Let's do it now."

"We can go in the van, save walking, eh?"

George parked on the slipway. "No need to get out, Colette. There's nothing wrong with the fenders. I stopped by on my way back to check."

"Then why the fuck are we sitting here, George?"

"You're angry."

"No, I'm not angry. I don't see the point in us talking if that's

189

what you have in mind."

"You've hardly said a word to me other than work since before your birthday."

"Are you surprised? I mean, it's not every day my lover tells me he's going to be a father."

His face tightened as Colette's words struck a nerve. "When I took you home you asked me to kiss you. You said not to part bad friends."

"That was a month ago. A lot has happened in my life since then."

Staring ahead at the slipway, he shook his head. "Not for me."

She rolled her eyes. "I don't have time for this. Just say what's on your mind."

He took a deep breath. "I want you to know I still love you."

"It's a bit late for that, George. I've moved on."

"When I left you, I drove home intending to tell mum about the baby, but she already knew. She told me she'd rather not have grandkids than have Jeanette as a daughter-in-law."

For the first time since she got into the van, Colette made eye contact with him. "Go on."

"I didn't go to the hospital. I haven't seen her since."

"What about her family?"

"They've made threats, but I can handle that."

She took a cigarette from his packet on the dashboard. "Why didn't you tell me this sooner?"

"You want to know what I did on your birthday?"

She sighed. "No, but I expect you're about to tell me."

"I bought your record and played it over and over in my room." He forced a smile. "Nearly drove mum nuts."

"I can imagine."

He leaned towards her and reached for her hand. "It's my turn to ask for a kiss."

She pecked his cheek. "Can't do more than that, George. Sorry."

He hammered his fists on the steering wheel. "You're sleeping with Leanne again!"

*

Leanne spread strawberry jam on two rounds of toast. "First breakfast on the balcony this year."

Placing a dish of hot croissants on the glass-topped table, Colette sat down. "I knew the sun would shine today."

"Thanks for your card, and your present is lovely."

"Sorry, perfume isn't very imaginative. What else could I buy someone who has everything?"

"Are you singing with the Shades at the Fermain Tavern tonight?"

"We've had this discussion several times, Leanne. If you don't want me to do it, I'll call John and cancel. It's just a guest appearance anyway, and I didn't know it was your birthday when I agreed to it."

"It doesn't matter. I'm not keen on being reminded every April sixth that I'm a year older."

"I'm only singing a couple of numbers. I'll ask John to put me on early, then we can go for a meal. What do you say?"

"Call him to pick you up. I'm not coming with you."

"What?"

Leanne topped up their mugs, added milk, and stirred for longer than necessary. "One of my old friends from Scotland is over. I haven't seen her in more than a year. We have a lot of catching up to do."

Colette frowned. "You've not said anything before. When did you hear?"

"You sound jealous, sweetheart. It doesn't suit you."

When Colette finished her usual Saturday housework, she prepared a special birthday meal. She hoped Leanne would be in a better mood when she returned from the market.

The meal was delicious, but their conversation was stilted. Placing Colette's empty plate on top of her own, Leanne stood up. "That was terrific, thank you, Colette. I'll do the washing up, it's half five, and you said John is coming at six."

"I only need to change and do my makeup. I feel terrible about tonight. Why don't you bring your friend, um, you didn't say her name…"

"It's Kay … Kay Ashton. I've known her for years."

"Well, why don't you bring Kay to the gig, I'd like to meet her?"

Leanne slammed the plates down on the table. "You think she doesn't exist, is that it?"

"For fuck's sake, Leanne! You've been bloody touchy since you came home. Why are you being so secretive about who's coming here tonight?"

"Excuse me. I don't need your permission to spend the evening with whoever I please."

When Colette's bedroom door slammed, Leanne flinched. She remembered another door slamming incident and what it led to. Not tonight though. She hated being furtive, but she had no choice.

"John's here … Colette, the van's here."

Colette came out of her bedroom, her face set in a scowl. "I heard you the first time."

"Hey, sweetheart. It's not what you think. I can't…"

"Fuck all to do with me, Leanne. Do whatever you want. You own the apartment anyway."

"What time will you be home, I'll have supper ready for you."

Colette swung round and let fly. "I'll be back whenever I fucking please. You don't own me. Whatever it is you're up to tonight, do it in your own bed. And, while you're about it, move your stuff out of my room."

*

While the others set up the lighting, Colette sat with John at a table near the stage. "That was crap."

"You or the Shades?"

"Me! I had a big bust up with Leanne. I couldn't get into it, I'm sorry."

"I did wonder when you sang the verses of your song out of sequence." He grinned. "It was only a sound check. You'll get it right when the punters come in."

"Life's a bitch, John."

"Take him back."

"You know?"

"It ain't no secret, babe."

She looked shocked. "He cheated on me! When Jeanette told him about the baby, he started seeing her again. He didn't have the guts to tell me."

John gave her a wry look. "That's what men do … didn't you know?"

Colette looked away. "That isn't funny."

"It wasn't meant to be, but you need to get your act together. You're sleeping with Leanne and…"

"You know that too?"

"George knows it, so I know it."

"I *was* sleeping with Leanne."

John raised his eyebrows. "Was?"

"Shit happens, John."

He nodded. "Listen! We all make mistakes. George thought he needed to take care of Jeanette. He didn't know she'd planned to have his baby."

"Are you saying she got pregnant on purpose?"

"If you don't believe me, ask Tiny. He's her cousin."

"I believe you. Go on."

"Tiny thinks it was her way of getting him back from you last September, and if you're not careful she'll succeed. I'll say no more, babe. It's your life."

Looking into the eyes of the man she once thought shallow and uncaring, she reached for his hand. "I hear what you're saying, John. Thank you."

"Come on, babe. The guys are on stage. We'll kick off with a couple of Dusty numbers, eh?"

*

Leanne heard a car drive into the courtyard and footsteps on the stairway. She opened the door and kissed his cheek. "It's good of you to come, Richard. Colette's not here, and I'm not sure what time she'll be back." She motioned across the hallway. "Please go through, both of you."

Richard Seabourne ushered a suited, business-like redhead into the living room. "I'm sorry we couldn't do this at a reasonable hour, Leanne. My sister is flying out in the morning."

"May I call you Leanne? I'm Kay Ashton. I'm on a brief visit to Guernsey looking at property. Your house would be perfect if it were for sale."

Leanne looked pensive. "I hadn't given it a thought until now, but we could discuss it before you leave if you like."

"Yes, let's do that. As you know, Richard called me weeks ago about Colette, so I thought I'd make time to hear some of her songs.

It's best she doesn't know that I'm interested until I'm sure it's what my company wants."

Leanne poured three glasses of Prosecco. "Yes, I understand the secrecy. But she thinks I'm having some sort of dalliance." She looked at Richard. "I had to lie to her, and that's something I never do."

"Let's hope she forgives you." He pointed to Colette's reel to reel tape on top of her amplifier in the corner. "That's her machine, is it?"

Kay had already spotted the recorder. "If you're happy for me to listen, I'll make sure to return the tape to the same position as it is now."

Leanne nodded. "I feel like a sodding criminal, but my girl deserves a break."

Kay glanced at her brother then back to Leanne. "Your girl?"

Richard returned the look. "None of our business, just the music, yes?"

Uncoiling the mains lead, Kay plugged it into a nearby wall socket, turned on the recorder and pressed play. "Ah, this is the one the Shades had a hit with, it's a good song." She keyed fast forward, stop, then play again. "And this was the B side." She listened to a few seconds of each track, wound the tape back to its original position, and turned the machine off. "It's rare to find such undiscovered talent. Your girl is very gifted, Leanne."

"Can you help her?"

"The music business is fluid. What might be a hit today could dive tomorrow. Colette's songs are not what the public is buying right now. However, the industry drives change; it wouldn't survive otherwise. I think she could have a great future and I'll get back to Richard as soon as I can. But it may take some weeks, I'm sorry."

"Thank you for being honest, Kay. What can I do in the meantime for her?"

Kay thought for a moment. "I shouldn't say this, but small independent labels that provide an alternative outlet for visionary performers and writers are flourishing. I'd encourage her to approach one of those."

Richard was listening with interest. "I know nothing about the music industry, but how does one go about setting up an independent label, Kay?"

"First you need an acoustically designed studio, professional mixing and recording equipment, a really good sound engineer, a ton of cash and—she looked at Leanne—at least one talented performer on your books!"

Leanne grinned. "Like my girl, you mean?"

*

Beth sat in an armchair knitting. "It's no good you sitting around here moping, son. Your dad would be up and doing something about it."

George slouched in front of the early evening TV. He liked The Prisoner and was fascinated with the spooky futuristic village and the giant floating ball that seemed to be controlled by an unseen force. But lately, his mind had been on other things. "She'll have nothing to do with me, mum."

"Talk to her." Beth smiled to herself. "Your dad wouldn't take no for an answer. That's how you came about."

"It's no good. She doesn't want to know." Remembering how he'd pounded the steering wheel when she could only kiss his cheek, he stared blankly at the TV. Then he imagined her in a passionate embrace with Leanne. "Anyway, she's seeing someone else."

Beth dropped her knitting into her lap. "Seeing someone else? What's that got to do with it? Dear oh dear, if your dad gave up on me just because I was seeing someone else, you'd be the son of a bank clerk. Oh no, your dad knew what he wanted and set about getting it. And so should you!"

George grabbed his coat from under the stairs. "You're a star, Ma," he shouted, as he picked up his van keys from the hall stand. "Wish me luck."

*

Checking her face and hair in a vanity mirror and straightening her mini-dress, Colette was ready to perform. John had nailed it; she really must get her act together. Stepping up onto the stage, she took her position at the microphone, looked back at Danny to count in, and felt more comfortable than she'd been during the sound-check.

As she sang, *I Only Want To Be With You*, she thought of George. At his party, he'd walked out, but their love for each other had grown into something special. Now it was gone.

Near the end of the third verse, she made a prearranged signal to John for an extended middle lead break. Moving away from the microphone to pick up her drink, she was out of the spotlight and could see the people at the back of the room. She'd only just been thinking of George, and there he was, leaning against a wall like a little boy lost. The refrain came around again. She took the microphone from its stand and moved away from the glare. She wanted to see him clearly while she finished the song.

"Not sure if I'll be back," she shouted to John over the applause.

"I saw him come in, babe. Stay cool."

She grabbed her coat, picked up her bag, and squeezed through the audience. "Hey, you look lonely."

"TV was shit, so I'm stalking my favourite pop star."

She donned her coat. "Well, I'm done here. If you can put up with me being miserable, we could have a quiet drink somewhere."

He looked surprised. "Am I about to wake up at any moment?"

"Daft sod! Come on. It's not been a good day for me, I need cheering up."

George started the van and headed for the car park exit. "Where to then?"

She couldn't help smiling at his boyish grin. "Let's just drive, see where it takes us, eh?"

He pulled onto the main road. "I'll take you on a magical mystery tour."

She made a face. "Oh, no! Leanne is constantly singing *Fool on the Hill* around the apartment."

He laughed. "That'd drive me mad. But I'm glad you're on your own tonight. Do you remember this road? It was dark last time."

"New Year's Eve, how could I forget?" She gave a satisfied nod. "You told me you loved me."

"That hasn't changed."

She moved in her seat to face him. "I've been a bitch, haven't I?"

"You said you wanted to go back in daylight."

"Yeah, I did, pet."

He settled back in his seat, a proud smile lighting up his face. "You called me 'pet.'"

She gave him a wicked look. "Slip of my tongue."

"No, nooo!" He made a fake grimace. "Please don't mention your tongue."

Colette laughed. She felt happier than she'd been for months. She shielded her eyes from the glare of a low April sun. "You said the sunsets over Lihou island were spectacular, will we get to our special place in time?"

"Only a few minutes left, we'll be just right I'd say." He swung the van into the tiny car park at L'Erée. Holding Colette's hand, he led her to the same spot on the shore where she'd reached for the stars. "Sorry, no blanket this time."

She giggled. "The spray soaked us, didn't it? The grass is dry, let's sit down."

He put his arm around her. "The sea is like a mill pond tonight. The reflection will be awesome."

She snuggled into George's embrace. "The sun is touching the island now. It looks like the whole sky is on fire."

"Only another couple of minutes before the magic happens."

"It's weird. Lihou is a black silhouette, yet everything else is pink, orange, and red."

"Don't look away! It's almost there."

She gazed in silence as the crimson orb sank slowly behind Lihou, its rippling twin rising to meet it. Then her eyes opened wide with amazement. "Wow ... just for a few seconds it looked as if the island was ablaze. I've never seen that before."

"It only happens here, Colette. Some people say it's a natural phenomenon, but I think it's mystical because of the legend."

The cool night air caused her to shiver. "I love spooky stories, tell me about it."

"They say that if a boy and girl kiss after watching the sunset over Lihou, they'll fall in love and never part."

She grinned. "George Bisson, you made that up just for a kiss."

He eased her back onto the grass, stroked a wisp of hair from her cheek, and looked into her eyes. "I did," he whispered, "I just want you to love me like you used to."

"I've never stopped loving you, pet." Feeling his rapid breaths on her cheek and his erection hard against her thigh, she eased him away. Unzipping his jeans, she caressed him. Slowly at first, then faster, until at last he let out a satisfied groan.

Breathing heavily with exhaustion, he closed his eyes. "That was incredible."

Smiling to herself, she took a tissue from her bag and pressed it into his hand. "Clean up, pet. We need to have a serious talk."

He sat up. "Damn, I left my ciggies in the van."

"I brought mine." Lighting two, she held one out for him. "So, what about us?"

Zipping up, he took the cigarette. "I had it all worked out in my head, but now I don't know."

"I'm listening."

He leaned forward hugging his knees, his long black hair closing like a curtain. "I'm scared, Colette."

She put her arm around his shoulders. "Hey, come on. We've got over that, haven't we?"

He looked up. "It's not that, you know it isn't"

"What then?"

"I'm not good with rejection."

"I don't understand."

"You're a terrific person; outgoing, clever, talented. I'm just boring old George. I had it all figured. Somewhere nice to live, sailing every summer weekend, curled up by the fire on cold winter evenings."

Shaking her head, she stroked his hair. "Real life isn't like that, pet."

He drew on his cigarette, blowing out the smoke forcefully. "Yeah, I know. It's just my imagination."

She gripped his hand. "But we could see how close we can get to it. Give it a go, eh?"

He turned to face her. "Just you and me?"

Her eyes glistened. "We could never get married, and I can't give you babies. But I'd never stop you seeing your child if that's what you wanted."

*

There were no lights on in the apartment when Colette arrived home. Remembering Leanne's suicide attempt on New Year's Eve, she rushed up the outside stairs.

She flipped the kitchen light switch. One empty Prosecco bottle stood by the bread bin, and on the draining board were three upturned wine glasses. *Three?*

Enough light shone through the serving hatch to see that the living room was deserted. She stood by the French doors. Something in the main house opposite had caught her eye. A backlit silhouette moved across the curtains of an upstairs room. She turned away. *Thank God, Leanne is unharmed.*

She went through her nightly routine of checking everything was safe. Her tape machine was plugged in. *I know I didn't leave it like that.*

She took a mug of coffee into her bedroom. Kicking off her shoes she sat down to remove her makeup. A note was propped up against her moisturiser jar:

I'll be over in the morning to collect the rest of my things.

I love you, sweetheart.

*

Colette couldn't bring herself to take breakfast on the balcony. That was something she did with Leanne. Coffee and a cigarette in the kitchen were all she could manage. She thought of George and Leanne, the two people in her life who loved her: *Do I love either of them? Do I know what love is?* Footsteps on the stairway and a shout interrupted her thoughts.

"Can I come in?"

"Since when do you need to ask?"

Leanne came into the kitchen. "Since I don't live here anymore."

"Coffee?"

"Yes please, white no sugar."

"For fuck's sake, Leanne. I do know how you take your coffee."

"Do you? When you went out yesterday, you didn't want to know me at all."

Colette slid Leanne's Fab Four mug across the counter. "I read your note when I got home."

"Yeah, well, the renovations were completed weeks ago. Best I get out of your way, eh?"

"Any point in me saying sorry?"

"You don't sound sorry, Colette."

"Weren't we both to blame?"

Leanne picked up her mug. "I'm dying for a cig. I smoked a whole packet during the night. I'll get some later and pay you back."

Colette motioned to her cigarettes and lighter. "Help yourself ... I put three wine glasses away."

Leanne glanced at the draining board. "Kay's brother was with her."

"Brother?"

"Look, I didn't lie to you last night, I just didn't tell the truth."

"Is there a difference?"

Leanne lit a cigarette and blew smoke towards the ceiling. "Kay's not an old friend. She works for a top record label."

"My reel to reel was plugged in."

"She wanted to hear your music."

"I could have played the bloody songs for her."

"She's a director of the company. She's not supposed to get involved with talent scouting."

Colette folded her arms. "How long did it take you to make all that up?"

"I knew you wouldn't believe me."

"Why should I? There's no way I can know."

Leanne spoke calmly. "Yes, there is, sweetheart. Ask Richard Seabourne. Kay Ashton is his sister."

Colette was taken aback. Leanne wouldn't mention a mutual acquaintance if it wasn't true. "What did she think of my songs?"

Leanne grinned. "She thought they were shit, but Richard's given me an idea."

Colette sighed. "You were right, I was jealous."

"That's only natural. After all, we were sleeping together."

"You can't move out of the apartment, Leanne."

"Oh, and why's that?"

"George is coming for dinner, and I'm crap at Yorkshire puddings."

"You're back together with George?"

"He came to the gig last night. We had a long talk and decided to see if we could make a proper relationship work."

"Living together you mean?"

"We haven't discussed that, but I guess so."

Leanne looked resigned. "I can't say I'm surprised."

"You're not upset?"

"No, not this time … have you had breakfast yet?"

"I couldn't face it."

"Nor me. Sit on the balcony, sweetheart. I'll make us some toast."

Sipping her coffee, Colette gazed at the elm tree. Last year, as Colin, she'd climbed it to fix up an antenna for the old bakelite radio he'd found. Now its new leaves were turning it from winter grey into spring green. The approach of summer, a new life with George. *Am I ready? Is this something I'm sure I want?*

Leanne placed a plate of buttered toast on the table and sat down. "Penny for them?"

Colette turned away from the tree. "Just thinking about all the things that have happened since I came here as Colin. If someone had told me then that a year later I'd be sitting here contemplating setting up home with a man, I'd never have believed them. But if I do get it together with George in a serious way, we'll need to find somewhere to live."

"I'll help you with that, but it can't be here in the apartment. I'm selling the house!"

"I'm not surprised, Leanne. It's a big place to live in on your own. Oh, shit! I'm sorry, I didn't mean…"

"It's alright. I'll get used to it. You don't sound so sure, though."

Colette thought about the freedom she'd enjoyed while not being seriously attached to someone. "It's a big step for me."

"And for George, too."

"Yeah, I'm not sure he'll cope with what I have to go through."

"Your physical change you mean?"

"The hormone treatment will be bad enough, but the surgery will be expensive, and I doubt my songwriting will bring in enough to pay for it. I couldn't expect George to help with that."

"You have a short memory, sweetheart."

"I don't understand."

"I once said I'd be there for you every inch of the way. Until you tell me you don't want me, that's where I'll be. As for somewhere for you and George to live, I have an idea. But there's something I need in return."

Colette grinned. "Bugger, I knew there'd be a catch, what is it?"

Leanne stood up. "Come here, all I need is a big hug and a promise that I'll always be your best friend."

Chapter 15 - Is it a boy or a girl?

George left work early and drove Colette to Route De Saumarez. Turning onto a freshly tarmacked road, he parked in the driveway of the first of eight newly built detached houses. He opened the front door and stood aside to allow her to enter. "I still can't believe Leanne is doing this for us, and it's fully furnished, too."

Colette stepped into the hallway, savouring the smell of fresh paint and new furnishings. "It was Derry Norman's show house. She bought it as an investment. If you like it, we can have it at a low rent."

"If *we* like it you mean."

"I've already seen it. I came here with Leanne a month ago. There's a garage for your van, and I'm sure you could make the garden nice."

George looked out of the kitchen window. "It'd take some work, but it's only May. There's still time to lay a lawn. I'll make a start at the weekend." He kissed her. "I could grow old here with you, Colette."

Grabbing his hand, she returned his kiss. "Come on, you still haven't seen upstairs. Then you can take me to your house, I need to tell your mum about me."

On the way to George's house, Colette couldn't help noticing that his boyish grin now looked much more grown up. Perhaps the idea of responsibility was having an effect. She listened while he planned his garden. Trees and shrubs for low maintenance and he'd build a shed. It was only right he should have his own space. After all, he'd readily agreed when she'd earmarked one of the bedrooms as a music room and studio.

"I've brought your favourite girl to see you, Ma," George shouted.

Beth came out of the kitchen wiping her hands on her pinafore. "What a lovely surprise, Colette. I'll make coffee for you. The kettle's just boiled."

"Thank you, Mrs Bisson. We've something important to speak to you about."

"Call me Beth, dear. Everyone does. Come through with me, and George will go over to the shop for biscuits."

Beth's kitchen wasn't spacious, but a small table covered with a flower-patterned plastic tablecloth gave it a homely feel. In the centre was a glass jar filled with chocolate digestives.

Colette sat down and tapped the jar. "You wanted George out of the way!"

Beth placed a mug of coffee on the table. "I don't have much time, so I'll come straight to the point. You setting up home with my George is the best thing that could happen to him. I want you both to be happy. If his dad were still alive, it'd probably be difficult for him to accept you, but I like you very much just as you are."

"You know then?"

"Course I do! I knew you were different the first time you came here with your hand all bandaged up. I couldn't put my finger on it at first, but it gradually fell into place."

"And that doesn't bother you, Beth?"

"Bother me? Don't be so daft. When you get to my age, you mull things over, get them into perspective so to speak. Why do people spend their lives with each other? I asked myself, if George's dad and me hadn't been blessed with a child, would we still have been together all those years? Course we would. So, having children isn't the answer. Then there's love, what is it? I thought about that for a long time, and I concluded that it's just being with someone who makes you happy. Simple as that."

"You are an amazing woman, Beth. George is lucky to have a mum like you."

"But there is something that does worry me."

Colette tried not to look alarmed. "Go on."

"You're not like other women, Colette … you're too nice!"

"A few people would disagree with you there, Beth."

"That's as may be. But my boy is going to be a father, and there are some who'd encourage you to give him up for the sake of the baby. He'll be back soon, so I'll say what I have to say and leave it at that. Whether it's with George or not, promise me you'll do what's right for you. Do that, and I know things will turn out as they are meant to be."

*

When Colette saw John's truck pull into the courtyard, she was surprised he wasn't in his usual working clothes this early on a

Saturday morning.

"Come in, John. Leanne's at the market, so we'll not be disturbed."

"What about George? Is he likely to turn up and find me in the arms of his betrothed?"

Colette smiled. "Are you ever serious?"

"You know me, babe. Look, I know I said on the phone I only need a couple of songs. Can I can take your tape? I'll copy and return it. The lads want enough tracks for an album."

"No problem, John. You'll be wanting a dozen or so. I'm not sure if there's enough good material for that. What's it all about?"

"After our second single flopped, the record company dumped us. We should've used another one of your songs, babe."

Removing her tape from the recorder, she slid it into a cover. "I've added a few more on this, mainly in the same theme as the one you had a hit with. You found another label yet?"

"I'm looking for an independent to sell our image, your style. The big boys don't want to take a chance on us."

She handed him the tape. "Well, let's hope my songs work for you."

"How are things with George? I heard Leanne bought dad's show house for you."

She rolled her eyes. "He's landscaping today. We're due to move in next Saturday. The eighth of June is my mum's birthday, so I can't forget, even if I tried."

"You don't sound keen, babe. Something wrong?"

She took a deep breath and sighed. "What have I done, John?"

"Hey, this is not like you. Come here you idiot, you need a hug." He took her in his arms. "Are you having second thoughts?"

"No, of course not."

"What's with the long face then?"

"I'll have to go through years of transition. Hormones and surgery to change my body shape. An operation to give me what a woman is born with, and a lengthy and painful recovery period. What sort of life will he have with me?"

"But he loves you. You can't let him down."

She shrugged. "He's a good man. I couldn't wish for better."

He kissed her cheek. "I don't like leaving you like this, but I have to go. We've no gig tonight, so Tiny and me are off to Jersey for a break."

She gave him a knowing look. "Sounds delicious, have fun."

He winked at her. "We will! Call if you need me, babe. Promise?"

"I'll be fine. Just nerves, that's all."

From the balcony, she watched John turn his truck in the courtyard. Her Saturday morning chores seemed pointless. She couldn't concentrate. Who cared if there was a film of dust on her dressing table? The rest of the apartment was neat and tidy, Leanne had seen to that. She lay on her bed staring at the ceiling.

John, the only man who understands me. A good friend, but never a lover, not my type. He's off for a weekend with Tiny, good for them.

George, the man I love more than anything else. We've discussed my medical needs, he's cool with that, supportive even. Why am I saying he couldn't cope? He's the most capable man I know!

Leanne! She cares for me, almost to the point of mothering me, but she doesn't care about her own kids. She didn't even call them in Scotland. Then suicidal when they chose their father.

Me? Mixed up kid... And that's a knock on the door ... I'm so engrossed with my self-pity I didn't even hear a car.

She forced herself to pull away from the comfort of her thoughts and go to the door. "What the fuck are you doing here, Jeanette?"

"I know I'm not welcome, but can I come in? I've walked from the bus stop."

"Jesus! In your condition? Get your arse in here. When are you due?"

"Clinic says next week. Mum says the week after. Gran thinks any time now."

"Shit! You'd better sit down. I'll make you a coffee. Can you have coffee?"

"I'd rather have tea if it's not too much trouble. Milk and two sugars, if you don't mind."

Colette motioned her through to the living room. "Yeah, right, um, tea. I'll put the kettle on."

"Is it alright if I sit at the table?" Jeanette shouted. "The chairs are higher, more comfortable for my tummy."

"Sure, whatever. Tea won't take a minute." Colette made a face at the closed serving hatch and wondered what this was all about. Jeanette wouldn't travel by bus across the island in her condition for nothing.

"I want to apologise for what I did at George's birthday party."

Pouring Jeanette's tea, Colette pulled another face. She placed the cup and saucer, her own coffee mug, and biscuits on a tray and carried it through to the living room. "You took your time, didn't you? That was last November."

"Mrs Cameron was right, I was just a kid. I've grown up a lot since then." She touched her tummy. "Case of having to."

"I appreciate your apology, but that's not the reason you're here, is it?"

Closing her eyes in pain, Jeanette took several deep breaths. "You can't have babies, Colette."

"Since when is that any of your business?"

"Since George told me you wouldn't stop him seeing his child."

Colette's jaw dropped. After all his promises, George had been to see her. "When did he tell you that?"

"Last night. He brought a pram he'd bought second hand. My uncle Peter told him I needed one."

"And you knew he wouldn't be with me today?"

"He told me he's doing the garden at your new house."

"So why are you here, Jeanette?"

"I want you to see what a real woman has to go through. I want

215

you to know what I'm giving him that you can't."

Colette shot to her feet. "You've not changed have you, Jeanette. Still the nasty piece of shit you've always been. Getting pregnant didn't work. George wants me, not you. Tough fucking luck."

Jeanette reached into her bag for a tissue. "I didn't mean it like that," she sniffled, "it came out all wrong. I'd better go."

Colette turned towards the kitchen. "Yes, I think you'd better, I'll call you a cab."

A car pulled into the courtyard below. Great, she could do with some moral support here. She rushed down the outside stairs to find Leanne gathering store bags from the back seat.

"This is a nice surprise, sweetheart. You don't often help me with the shopping."

"We've got company, Leanne."

"Really? I don't see a car, who is it?"

"Jeanette. She came by bus."

"Oh! Did she now? Her baby is due. She'll have hatched some sort of plan to get George back."

While Colette put the shopping in the kitchen, Leanne went directly into the living room. "I know what your game is, Jeanette, and it won't work. I'm taking you home."

Breathing deeply, Jeanette held her stomach with both hands. "I just need a minute Mrs Cameron. I don't feel well."

Leanne looked more closely at her. "When did your contractions start?"

"The first one was this morning soon after mum went out."

"What time was that?"

"Before nine. She always gets the early bus to the market on Saturdays."

Glancing at the wall clock, Leanne frowned. "Over four hours ago! So, you thought it'd be a good idea to jump on a bus, come here, and make Colette feel fucking awful, did you?"

Jeanette moaned with pain. "I was alright until I slipped and banged my tummy coming up the stairs."

Leanne sat down. "Shit, that's not good. Did you tell Colette what happened?"

"She wouldn't know what to do. She's not a..."

"That's enough of that young lady."

Colette stopped eavesdropping in the hall and burst into the living room. "Honestly, Leanne. I had no idea."

"Never mind that, we need to get Jeanette into your bedroom, then we'll call an ambulance. Go grab some clean towels and spread them on your bed, I don't know if her water's broken."

"Her what?"

"Just do it. I'll explain later."

Gathering several bath towels from the airing cupboard, Colette layered them in the centre of her bed.

Supporting Jeanette as best she could, Leanne appeared at the bedroom door. With extra pillows under her head, they made her as comfortable as possible.

When Jeanette screamed with another contraction, Colette began to panic. "Do you want me to call an ambulance now, Leanne?"

"I want to see if she's dilated. Leave the room if you're squeamish."

Folding back Jeanette's skirt, Leanne next pulled down her panties. "Sensible girl, you've used a pad." Lifting her knees, she gently eased them apart. "Now let's see how near you are ... Oh, shit!"

Colette fidgeted by the door. "What's the matter, Leanne?"

"Get on that phone now. Tell them the baby's head is showing."

While Colette called the hospital, Leanne held Jeanette's hand and told her when to relax, and when to breathe deeply.

Colette came back into the bedroom. "They said ten minutes, will she be alright?"

"I think so. Her contractions are close together and longer, she's fully dilated, too. Just to be on the safe side, I think we should prepare."

"What can I do, Leanne?"

"We probably won't need them, but I want you to fetch a couple of things."

"Fuck, what if I get it wrong?"

"Don't worry, Colette. I'm not going to ask for boiling water and a sharp knife like they do in the movies. Fetch an empty bowl for the... just fetch a bowl and some more clean towels, yeah? Then come back and hold her hand, I need to be ready for the delivery.

It'll not be long now."

While Leanne spread a clean towel ready for the baby to fall into, Colette held Jeanette's hand wondering what the fuck she was doing helping to deliver George's ex-girlfriend's baby.

Leanne gave Colette an anxious glance. "The cord is over the baby's head."

Colette knew she was out of her depth, but was desperate to support Leanne. "What can you do about it, is it serious?"

Leanne bit her lip and tried again to move the cord aside. "No, it's too tight, we'll have to deal with it when the baby comes out."

"We?"

There was no time for Leanne to explain. "It's happening … Push, Jeanette, push. Come on girl. You can do it. Push as hard as you can. Now. Do it now."

Jeanette groaned, breathed extra deeply, then yelled.

Leanne caught the baby in the towel, unwrapped the cord from its face, wiped its nose between finger and thumb to remove any mucus, then sighed with relief that it was breathing.

Colette stared at the tiny wrinkled, blue-faced, thing covered in bloody slime. When it gave its first cry, she wanted to wail too. She'd never experience such a wonderful thing as childbirth.

Leanne carefully wrapped the baby in a soft hand towel. "I want Jeanette sitting up with pillows behind her, sweetheart. She needs to hold the baby as quickly as possible to keep it warm."

"I'm onto it. Is it a boy or a girl?"

Leanne smiled. "You'll know soon enough." She gently placed the baby in Jeanette's arms. "Congratulations, you have a beautiful, healthy baby girl. But be careful, the cord is still attached. The medics will deal with it when they get here, and we have a bowl for the placenta if it arrives before they do."

Nuzzling her new-born daughter to her breast, Jeanette undid her blouse buttons and leaned forward. "Can you undo my bra please, Colette? I think she's thirsty."

Leanne helped Jeanette to bring her baby to the nipple. "A baby's first feeds are important," she said, more as enlightenment for Colette than the new mother. "Mum's first milk is Colostrum. It contains all the things a baby needs to keep it healthy."

With its siren still wailing, the ambulance screeched to a halt in the courtyard. The midwife rushed up the stairway, followed by a nurse.

Leanne opened the door. "I'm afraid the baby couldn't wait for you." She motioned towards Colette's bedroom. "Just through there."

"Bloody traffic … you can leave her to us now. Come on Molly, second one today, no rest for the wicked."

In the kitchen, Colette put the kettle to boil and loaded the cafetière. "I've been thinking, shouldn't we have called her mother?"

"I asked her while you were collecting towels. She didn't want her mum or George."

"What? You asked her if she wanted George here?"

"Don't get angry. Think about it, sweetheart. When he finds out that his daughter was born in your bed, he'll wonder why he was excluded. Now you have an answer to that. She didn't want him here. He can't blame you."

Colette relaxed. "You're right, and you were brilliant with the baby stuff."

"Women tend to know these things. That's why I was pleased when you did your bit."

Colette smiled. "Yeah, it was special, wasn't it?"

They both turned at the sound of footsteps on the stairway. Leanne opened the door to the ambulance driver.

"Sorry to bother you, but I've had a call on the radio. As soon as the midwife's finished here, we've another visit to make, and it's urgent."

The nurse came out of the bedroom and hurried down to the courtyard.

The midwife stopped by the kitchen door. "Well done you two, a perfect delivery. Mother and baby are in good shape. You should call your doctor to visit as soon as possible. We'll dispose of the placenta. Must dash, cheerio."

Colette looked at Leanne. "What the hell do we do now?"

"Well, I guess we've got a lodger, at least until someone comes to collect her. I'll call her mother. Go on through and see how the baby is."

It seemed odd to Colette to be tentatively opening her own

bedroom door. "Is there anything you need, Jeanette? A hot drink or something?"

"No, I'm fine now, Colette. My little cherub is still having her feed."

"Leanne's calling your mum to get you home."

Jeanette nodded. "Thanks, best thing I suppose."

"You don't sound happy about that."

"You don't know my mother. She's not the nicest person."

Colette sat on the edge of the bed. "I'm sorry, I shouldn't have said."

"She drinks … a lot. Down the pub most of the time."

Colette felt uneasy. "Must be awful for you."

"The men she brings home, a different one nearly every night."

"That bad, eh?"

"Yeah, that bad." She stroked the baby's downy head. "Me and my little girl will be alright, we'll find somewhere."

Colette rushed into the kitchen. "Did you get through yet?"

"Still no answer, why?"

"Jeanette's staying here."

Leanne swung round. "You're out of your fucking mind, girl."

"Things are bad at home, she just told me."

"Oh yeah? What exactly did she tell you?"

"Her mother drinks heavily and takes men home. That's not the sort of place for a new-born baby, Leanne."

"She's piling it on, sweetheart. She's out to get George."

"I don't give a shit what she's out for. I just watched a new life enter this world. I'd never forgive myself if anything happened to it."

"Settle down Colette. The phone is still on at the show house. I'll call George and tell him what's happened. He'll know if she's telling the truth."

With her daughter still at her breast, Jeanette was dozing. When Colette sat on the edge of the bed again, she opened her eyes. "You think I'm making it up, don't you?"

"It did cross my mind, yes."

Jeanette pulled her blouse together. "She's finished her feed. Do you want to hold her?"

Colette drew back in fright. "You're kidding! I know nothing about babies."

"You know more than you think. You saw her being born. Just hold your arm like I'm doing to support her head."

Despite an overwhelming urge to flee, Colette took George's daughter in her arms. "I can't believe I'm doing this. She's beautiful. What are you going to call her?"

"I haven't decided yet. Gran wants Elizabeth. Mum doesn't care. I'm open to suggestions."

Colette looked up. "What about 'Leanne?' She brought her into the world."

Jeanette thought for a moment. "I like the sound of that, but not as a first name. You were here too, Colette. What's your middle name?"

"You're unlucky with that. I don't have one."

Leanne came into the room grinning. "Well, there's a sight I never thought I'd see."

"We were thinking about baby names Mrs Cameron. I'd like her middle name to be Leanne if that's alright."

Leanne tickled the baby's chin. "I'd be honoured, Jeanette, thank you. Have you decided on a first name?"

Jeanette smiled. "I have … she's to be called Colette."

Chapter 16 - A place of magic and mystery

When George's van skidded to a halt in the courtyard, Colette rushed down to meet him. She didn't want raised voices in the apartment.

"What am I doing here, Colette?"

"Your one-hour-old daughter is in my bed with her mother. That's why you're here."

"I meant, what am I doing *here*. What's going on?"

"She just turned up on my doorstep, then nature took its course. What the fuck was I supposed to do? Shove her out onto the street to give birth? We can talk about it later, go and see your new baby."

"Come in with me, Colette. I can't do this on my own."

"Jeanette is expecting just you. It wouldn't be right."

"I'll ask Leanne. She'll come in with me."

"She's out buying baby clothes, and other stuff for Jeanette."

George looked puzzled. "How long is Jeanette staying here?"

"Later, George. Just go and see her. I'll be in the garden. I've some thinking to do."

Colette paused by a rose covered pergola. She closed her eyes and breathed in the heady fragrance. Jeanette wanted her daughter to have a father. Who could blame her? What sort of life would little Colette have without George to hold her up high and swing her around, laugh at her first steps, read her stories at bedtime, and teach her to ride a bike? Sail every inch of the islands and much of the French coast, too. Just as his dad had done with him?

If I were Jeanette, would I move heaven and earth to get George to be a full-time father for my daughter? To provide a home and a loving environment, a safe place for his tiny seedling to grow and blossom into a beautiful flower? You bet your sweet life I would!

"I'm blown away. She's so small."

Colette swung round. "New-born babies usually are, George."

He grinned. "Oh, so you're an expert now, are you?"

"I pick things up quickly, especially when my lover's baby is born in my bed!"

"I feel so bloody helpless! I can't do anything for Jeanette without upsetting you, Colette. But you and Leanne are fussing over her like mother hens."

"Would you rather your daughter lived under the same roof as Jeanette's mother?"

"I'll find a flat or something for them."

She took George's arm. "Let's walk. What I have to say is best said under the elm tree. It greeted me when I arrived here, it watched over me when I didn't know who I was, and it'll nod and say, 'take care, my friend,' when I walk down the driveway for the last time."

George looked worried. "What are saying? You can't…"

"Shh, we're nearly there." She looked up. "Did you know I climbed up it once? Inside the foliage, it's like another world. A place of magic and mystery."

He gazed up at the lofty old elm, his eyes glistening. "Like the sunsets over Lihou island, the legend." He took her in his arms. "Please don't do this Colette, I love you so very much."

Slipping her hands under his hair, she pulled him close. "It's the only way, pet. I can't be part of your life now."

He shook his head. "No, bloody no … you can't do this to me. What about our future? We had it all planned out."

"Your future is with your daughter. She needs you. Kiss me, and make it a kiss that we'll both remember always."

Finally, she eased him away. "Wherever I am, every New Year's Eve I'll whisper, 'I love you.' Promise me you'll do the same."

He brushed back her long blonde hair. "At the stroke of midnight every year. I promise."

With a heavy heart, she watched him walk to his van and drive away. He didn't look back.

Leanne's car swung into the courtyard. She parked beside the garage doors and beckoned to Colette. "Help me with the bags, sweetheart. I passed George on the drive, everything alright?"

Colette sighed. "No! But it's sorted. I need us to talk."

"Shit, you look terrible! Here, take my keys and go into the main house. I'll come over when I've shifted this lot. I'd rather not air our personal stuff with Jeanette listening."

Before making coffee, Colette boiled the kettle twice; it hadn't been used for weeks. Sitting at the kitchen table, she recalled the day she arrived in Guernsey as Colin. Life was less complicated then: The bustle of Leanne preparing a meal. Playing 'Mousetrap' with the twins. James shouting during some silly domestic quarrel.

She crossed to the sink, tore off a sheet of kitchen roll, damped it under the tap, and wiped off her lipstick. Unclasping her butterfly necklace, she laid it on the countertop with her earrings and wristwatch. She took a pair of scissors from the cutlery drawer and stepped over to a mirror. Colin had arrived with nothing. He'd leave with nothing but fond memories.

Leanne burst into the kitchen. "What the fuck are you doing, Colette?"

"Colin needs a haircut."

"Shit! Sit down. We have to talk this through. And give me those sodding scissors before you do something you might regret."

"I can't go on being Colette. It's too painful."

"So, you'll change back to Colin, and everything will be fine, eh? You forget all the people who accepted you. John, the guys at work … me!"

"I'm not going back to work."

"Oh! You're going to let me down, too, are you? I thought you were better than that. Obviously, I was wrong."

"I can't be around George. It'd destroy me, and him. I'm going home."

"Your home is here, with me."

"You're selling the house."

"We'll live somewhere. Now listen, Colette…"

"Colin."

"Does it matter what I call you?"

"I guess not."

"I understand how you must feel, but hacking off your hair will achieve nothing. If you do want it short, get it done at a hairdresser."

"That makes sense."

"Good! Now, I take it you've finished with George?"

"He's hurt, but he should be with his daughter."

"Fine. You won't need your house now, will you?"

"No, it'd be ideal for Jeanette and the baby, though."

"Exactly! George can move them in with the van. It'll be up to him if he lives there with them. I think he will."

"He'll need time off work."

"He deserves a holiday. I'll give him an extra week with pay."

"So, you want me to continue at the yard?"

"Just until next weekend as Colette. After that, it's up to you what you want to do and who you want to be."

"You know I can't let you down, Leanne. But I'd like to stay here in the main house. I don't seem to have a bedroom right now."

"If George wants to be in the apartment with Jeanette and his daughter, I'll move over here, too. At least until they've gone. What do you say … Colette?"

She managed a smile. "It's a deal. Let's fetch some bedding from the apartment. I want to hold the baby again."

*

Monday morning staff meetings were an important, and usually upbeat, event. But breaking the news to Bob and Frank that she was leaving at the end of the week was not easy. She couldn't tell them the real reason, but their consoling comments indicated that they'd probably guessed. Later in the morning, Leanne called her into the office.

"How's it going out on the shop floor, sweetheart?"

Pulling up a chair, Colette lit a cigarette. "The lads are cut up that I'm leaving, but happy for George. They're worried about their jobs; the two cruisers we've built on spec are nearing completion, and still no buyers."

Leanne fidgeted with a ruler. "I've re-advertised them in three boating magazines. I'd hate to have to do it, but if that doesn't work, I may well have to reduce the workforce. That's between us, right?"

"My lips are sealed. Seems odd without George here."

"He's preparing the house today. Jeanette and the baby are moving in tomorrow. If you miss him that much, I could call him in on Wednesday?"

Colette forced a smile. "I hope it goes well for them. I'll probably regret it when I'm old and grey, but I think I did the right thing."

"Best not dwell on it, eh? Richard Seabourne called earlier about the house. His sister wants to make an offer. He's coming here this morning."

"I'll make myself scarce then." Colette stubbed out her cigarette and headed for the door. "Talk of the devil, here he is."

Richard stepped into the office. "Nice to see you again, Colette. How's the music coming along?"

"Um, fantastic thanks. Couldn't be better. I must dash."

Richard turned to Leanne. "That's unlike Colette?"

"She's going through a bad patch."

"Well, I shan't pry. She's an interesting girl though. I've always liked her."

Leanne grinned. "Liking women? That's a first, Richard."

He winked. "You know me, Leanne. But I do like Colette. Ah well, down to business. Kay wants me to arrange a survey and valuation of your property, usual thing. Is that alright?"

"Yes, of course. Just let me know when, so I can be there."

"Good, that's settled. I mentioned on the telephone that I'm interested in buying the boatyard. I know it's not doing well, but I believe it has potential. Have you thought any more about it?"

Leanne opened her desk drawer. "Here's a recent inventory and a brief financial summary. I can't keep ploughing money into it with no return. So, yes, I'd be willing to sell, and I know you'd be fair."

While Richard Seabourne studied several pages, Leanne made coffee.

"I'm sorry, I didn't bring my briefcase, would you have a scrap of paper?" He took a gold fountain pen from his top pocket, wrote a figure on a sheet of typing paper Leanne gave him, folded it, and put it on her desk. "What would you say this place is worth as a going concern, Leanne? Including the two unsold boats, of course."

"I have no idea, Richard. I'd not even thought about it until you called."

"Well, if the books tally with your summary, my offer is on that piece of paper. Negotiable of course."

Leanne unfolded the note. "Good God. I would never have thought that much."

"Shall I send my accountants to take a look?"

"Please do … I'm overwhelmed. You've just taken a huge weight off my mind."

"So, if all is in order, you'd be prepared to go ahead?"

Leanne sat back. "Give me a couple of days to think about it. Your offer is very generous, but I want to be certain in my mind that I'm doing the right thing. I'm sure you understand, Richard."

"I do indeed. If you're worried about the staff, I can assure you I'd keep them on. Colette is an exceptional manager."

"And if she doesn't come with the business, does your offer still stand?"

Richard's eyes twinkled. "Of course it does. Do you have other plans for her?"

"Yes, I might do. She needs to get away, and so do I."

"For a holiday, or something more permanent?"

"Oh, I don't know. Just away from Guernsey for a bit."

He thought for a moment, took out his pocket book, and unfolded a brochure. "Take a look at this, Leanne. It's a property owned by a popular entertainer who's already moved to America. A friend of mine in the trade thought I might be interested. It's not officially on the market yet. It would suit you and Colette perfectly."

Leanne took the leaflet and laughed. "It's a bloody boatyard,

Richard."

"I can see you're amused, but think about it. Boating on the Norfolk Broads is mainly holiday hire. It's in a good location, and best of all it has a large house and a fully equipped recording studio. I was interested in it for that fact alone. You know I've been looking into starting an independent label."

A plan was already forming in Leanne's mind. "When is it being advertised?"

"My contact tells me next Monday, one week from today. I could arrange a viewing before then if you wanted."

Leanne studied the brochure again. "There's no asking price, any idea?"

"I did make enquiries. It's almost exactly the figure I wrote on that note."

Leanne's jaw dropped. "That's very affordable. Why is it valued so low?"

"Even though it has a good stock of hire craft, they are old boats, and the business has suffered from bad management. And, of course, land in East Anglia is nowhere near as expensive as in Guernsey."

"Yes, arrange it for me, please. Even if it's not what we want, the break will do us good."

"When would you like to go?"

"Next weekend, Saturday. Do you think that's possible?"

"For you dear girl, anything is possible. Consider it done."

Leanne looked excited. "I can't wait to tell Colette. I'll book flights and a hire car."

*

Colette pushed her plate aside. Leanne's cottage pie was usually a treat, but the thought of George just across the courtyard with Jeanette was getting to her. "I'm sorry, I'm just not hungry."

Leanne scraped uneaten remains from her own plate to join those on Colette's. "The birds will have a good feed. It must be this flaming June heat. I'm sure it's worse than last year."

"Every sodding thing is worse than last year, and I'm not just talking about the temperature. Will you be sad when the house is sold?"

"No, too many hurtful memories. I'll miss the apartment though. We had some good times, didn't we?"

Colette looked towards the kitchen window. On the balcony opposite, George was holding his daughter. She turned back to Leanne. "No point living in the past. I have to get on with my life."

"Where will you go?"

"I won't be staying in Guernsey."

Leanne offered Colette a cigarette. "I have to fly to the mainland on Saturday. Do you want to come with me? The change of scenery will do us both good."

"Oh? … Where to?"

"There's a house I've got my eye on in Norfolk. I'd value your opinion."

"You do know I'm changing back to Colin after I leave work on

Friday, don't you?"

Leanne pretended nonchalance. "It doesn't bother me, sweetheart. You must do what you think best. So, do I book two hotel rooms or one?"

"Do you mean am I coming with you?"

"I know you'll come with me. You're as pissed off with hanging around here as I am. But I need to know if you want a separate room."

Colette took her time. She missed the warmth of an embrace, the safeness of being in someone's arms. "I don't think Colin will mind sharing."

Leanne grinned. "Now I am looking forward to Saturday. What about Colette?"

"What about her? After Friday, she won't exist."

Leanne reached across the table. "You're Colette now though, sweetheart. Shall we have an early night?"

Grasping Leanne's hand, Colette took a deep breath. "After what we've been through the last few days, I think we both need each other, don't we?"

Chapter 17 - I've always been your little girl

Colin gazed out of the aircraft window at the windswept landscape of the Norfolk Broads below. As a child, he'd holidayed here with mum and dad; fishing, and exploring the network of natural waterways and broad artificial lakes formed over centuries of peat harvesting.

It was difficult acting like Colin again after being Colette for so long. He'd made an effort to stop swinging his hips, and all the other female mannerisms he'd unconsciously adopted. But no matter how hard he tried, his voice still sounded feminine.

With no time to visit a hairdresser, he'd tied his hair in a ponytail and Leanne had trimmed the ends. He wasn't sure that short hair would be right for him now anyway. The scissors scene in the kitchen was a moment of despair. He'd got over that. As Colette was still a part of him, her jeans, tee shirt, and deck shoes were comforting to wear. An androgynous look seemed a perfect compromise.

He wondered what mum and dad were doing. Even though today was her birthday, his mother would be serving in the local bakery; a job she'd taken on to make ends meet when he'd started school. Father would be on light duties at the fire station recovering from a back injury. In her most recent letter, mother had written of his possible retirement due to ill health.

Leanne nudged him; the no smoking and fasten seatbelts sign had flashed on. "You looked as if you were in a world of your own."

"I was thinking about home. It'd be nice to see mum and dad again."

"We're not going back until Tuesday. How far is Ipswich?"

He grinned. "Forty miles or so, about an hour by car. Do you think we could?"

Leanne reached for Colin's hand. "Well, we were sightseeing tomorrow, but I'd be just as happy meeting your parents. We could take a birthday present for your mum, too. Let's do that instead, eh?"

*

Colin soon identified their destination on the east side of Barton Broad; the hire car company had supplied a map of the area with the brand-new red Ford Cortina. "We're coming up to Woodfield now, Leanne. Take the first turning left. After about half a mile there's a track to the boatyard."

Leanne gave Colin a sideways glance. "Are you sure you have that map the right way up? It seems like I've been driving around in circles for the last few miles!"

"With seven rivers and few road bridges, there's no direct route to anywhere on the Broads."

"Oh! So, which one are we heading for?"

"The river Ant. It runs south through Barton Broad and into the river Bure. I know this part of Norfolk. Dad used to hire a boat from Martham for our holidays."

Leanne parked by an imposing but tired looking old house. "Well, I'm glad one of us knows where we are. This looks like the back of beyond to me. We're early for the estate agent. Let's have a poke around until she arrives."

While Leanne gathered her bag and locked the car, Colin tried the front door, then peered through windows until she joined him. "Looks like it's furnished. That'd save you some money."

"According to Richard's contact, everything in the house goes with the property."

Shielding his eyes against the strong June sunshine, Colin pointed towards a concrete surfaced lane running between two barns. "It looks like the way to the boatyard over there. Come on, Leanne. That's my territory."

While Leanne met the secretary cum hire manager in a bright and cheerful office, Colin chatted boats and boating with an elderly craftsman in the large but ramshackle boatshed.

Three of the eight traditional wooden cruisers belonging to the yard were tied up at the staithe, and one stood on a launching cradle at the top of the slipway. Knowing that Broads fleets often had recognisable registrations, Colin was not surprised that these boats' names all started with the letter D; Doreen, Daisy, Dawn, and Deborah.

While he was contemplating the names of the other four, Leanne approached. "What do you think, sweetheart?"

"You know me, anything to do with boats and I'm hooked. From what I can see of the fleet, a lot of work needs doing to bring them up to scratch. The boatshed is well equipped, though." He pointed to a grubby Luton bodied Ford Transit van next to a grey Ferguson tractor. "It's odd that several of the items have 'for sale' notices on them."

Leanne shuffled some paperwork. "It seems the owner wants a quick return on some of the movables. Looking at this list the secretary gave me, I think we should decide before there's nothing left to buy, eh?"

Colin looked puzzled. "We?"

"Yes, we! You and me. Like it or not, If I buy this place, you're coming with me, right? Now, let's go see that recording studio of yours."

"I don't get it, Leanne! This is a boatyard, isn't it?"

She took his arm. "A boatyard that's full of surprises. Come on. The estate agent should be here by now."

A slim middle-aged brunette in a flowery summer dress and clutching a clipboard was waiting by the house. She shook hands with Leanne and peered at Colin over her sunglasses. "Good afternoon Mrs Cameron, I'm Lisa Godwin. Our mutual contact, Richard Seabourne, is a good friend. I'm so pleased to meet you both. You must be Colette. Do I need to show you the boatyard?"

Leanne glanced at Colin. "No, we were early, so we had a look around. We'd like to see the house though, especially the studio."

"Well, let's do that first, it's in the barn to the left of the lane."

Following Lisa across the hard standing, Leanne caught hold of Colin's arm. "Richard doesn't know you've changed back. It'll make things easier if you're Colette while Lisa is here. Is that alright?"

Colin halted and turned to Leanne. "I don't believe this. You know how I feel."

"Oh, come on Colin, just while Lisa's here. I know you're hurt, but you shouldn't have to explain something so personal to a bloody estate agent."

Colin rolled his eyes, but he knew Leanne was right. "Just while she's here. Not a minute longer, and I mean that!"

"Right, Colette … Lisa is waiting for us."

Entering the spacious well-equipped recording studio, Colette crossed over to the control booth. She admired the professional mixing desk and drooled over the multi-track recording equipment. Returning to where Leanne was talking to the estate agent, she paused by guitars and amplifiers set up ready to play. She thought about the Gibson that George had bought her, and the Christmas message, *Je T'aime,* on a card still inside the case. *Will I ever stop thinking about George every time I see a guitar? Will I have to give up playing myself just to be free of the memory?* She tried not to sound miserable. "I'm impressed. Do the instruments come with the studio?"

Lisa grinned. "I'm afraid not, young lady. I've known the owner since he bought the property three years ago. He allows my daughter's all-girl band to rehearse here. I expect that will change when a new owner takes over, though."

Leanne gave Colette a secret smile. "Not necessarily, Lisa. I mean, what's a recording studio without musicians? We'd like to look at the house now."

Unlocking the front door, Lisa stepped inside. "As you know, everything in here goes with the property. Some of the furniture is dated, but on the whole, it's homely. The kitchen is modern, but both bathrooms need refurbishing, and you may want to have the ancient plumbing checked out."

Entering the roomy foyer, Leanne sniffed the air. "I expected the house to smell fusty, Lisa. Is someone living here?"

"Emily, the housekeeper, keeps the place spick and span. Her husband William is the gardener. If you buy the property, you might want to keep them on. They're absolute treasures. You would have passed their cottage just along the track from the main road."

"Yes, I saw it, a lovely place. Just like a chocolate box picture. An arch of roses over the front gate, too. I'm beginning to like Norfolk."

Lisa gave her estate agent's guided tour around the house pointing out many Victorian features, but when she came to the formal dining room with its oak panelling and decorative plasterwork, she looked downcast. "I'll miss this place, Leanne. The owner wasn't just a client, he became a good friend, too. He always invited my husband and me for special occasions. We weren't sure if you'd reserved accommodation. Emily always keeps one room prepared for visitors." She glanced at Colette. "I could ask her to make up another if you want to stay."

Colette ran a finger along a marble mantlepiece. "I'd love to, but you've booked the hotel, Leanne."

Leanne prodded the maroon leather seat of one of a dozen dining chairs surrounding a polished mahogany table. "Is there a telephone I could use? I'll need to cancel our reservation at the Rushmore."

Lisa took her diary from a side pocket of her bag. "I know the manager there, I could do that for you if you like. And I'll ask Emily to prepare another room."

"That's kind, but the one room already made up will be fine." Leanne gave Colette another secret smile. "We like to share, don't we, sweetheart."

A few minutes later, Lisa returned. "The manager at the Rushmore says you owe him a drink, and he'd be delighted to meet you if you do buy the property. Emily said she'll cook something and bring it over early this evening if that's alright. It's Sunday tomorrow so I won't be in the office. Please do take another look around, and I'll come to see you here on Monday morning. If you do decide to buy, I'll cancel the advertising."

Leanne looked up from her notes. "I think we've already decided, Lisa. But I'll confirm on Monday. Just a thought, if I wanted that van down by the boatshed, could I buy it straight away?"

Lisa shook hands with Leanne. "Agree on a price with the yard office, and it's yours. Have a lovely weekend both of you."

Leanne waved Lisa off then returned to the kitchen where Colin had found a boating magazine to read. "That was nice, sweetheart."

He looked up. "Yeah, I liked her, and you don't have to drive back to Norwich tonight."

"I didn't mean Lisa. It was nice calling you Colette again."

"Stop it, please Leanne. It's just a name, no big deal."

"Oh, come on, Colin. When you spotted those instruments, I saw the look on your face. You were thinking about George."

He tossed the magazine onto the table. "I'm trying to forget him, Leanne. But every time I see a guitar, I think of the Gibson he bought me."

"He bought Colette you mean."

Colin stared at Leanne. Her words had hit home. Denying his true feelings was becoming painful. "No, he bought it for me. I'm still Colette. I'm using my old name now, that's all." He raised his hand to his chest. "But nothing's changed in here."

Leanne stood behind him and stroked his hair. "Oh, sweetheart, why can't you just be yourself then?"

"Because I can't! Not until I've left Guernsey, anyway."

She kissed his cheek. "Could you be happy here with me?"

Colin shrugged. "I'm short on options right now, Leanne."

She knelt beside him and took his hands in hers. "That's not what I asked you. I want you to be with me wherever we end up, and here seems as good a place as any. I'm not asking you to love me. I'm asking if you'd be happy with me."

He leaned forward and kissed her. "Happiness isn't something I can even consider right now. Give me time to sort my head out. See how it goes, eh?"

She drew him close. "Thank you, sweetheart. I know it'll work out for us. When will Colette be coming back for good?"

"I'll talk to mum tomorrow. I owe her that at least. The morning we leave Guernsey to come back here I'll be Colette again, I promise."

*

Colin threw back the covers, kissed Leanne's cheek, and crossed to the window.

Leanne yawned, sat up, and arranged a pillow behind her. "Looks like another beautiful morning. What are you looking at, sweetheart?"

"It's Sunday, the first full day for most of the families enjoying their boating holiday. Every proud dad a captain for a week or a fortnight, not a care in the world."

Leanne crossed to the dressing table and picked up a hairbrush. "You sound sombre! Come here, and I'll brush the tangles out of your hair."

He sat on the edge of the bed. "Yeah, it's a big day for me."

"I'd be happier if you called your mother. After fifteen months away, It'll be a shock for her just turning up on the doorstep."

"She'd only put on a banquet and invite my uncles and aunts. I need to talk to her alone."

Leanne slipped off her nightdress. "Well, you know her best. Emily brought some bread and eggs yesterday, Let's grab some breakfast and get on the road. The sooner you get it over with, the sooner you'll relax."

Colin never tired of admiring Leanne's mature figure. She'd put on some weight around her tummy recently, but that only added to her appeal. He sighed and wondered if Colette would ever be half as attractive naked.

Apart from stopping at a corner shop to buy chocolates for Colin's mother, the drive down to Ipswich was uneventful.

Leanne pulled into a parking space only a few yards from his house. "It's now or never, sweetheart. Do you want me to wait in the car?"

Drawing in a deep breath, he braced himself. "I'd rather you come in with me. You can keep dad busy while I talk to mum in the kitchen."

Before Colin took a step towards his home, his father came along the path. "Good God, you're a sight for sore eyes, son. I'm just on my way to work. I thought I was seeing things. That can't be my boy getting out of that shiny new Cortina I said to myself, but it is you. Your mother will be as pleased as punch." He looked into the car. "Who's this then, a girlfriend?"

"It's good to see you, dad. I've mentioned Leanne in my letters."

"Well, you're very welcome, Leanne. Go right in the both of you. I only wish I could stay, but my shift starts in fifteen minutes. If you'd called first, I could have swapped with one of the lads. You know how it is, Colin."

"Yeah, I do, dad. I won't leave it so long next time."

Collecting the birthday present from the back seat, Leanne locked the car door and came round to the near side where Colin was watching his father hurry away. "What shall I do now, sweetheart? I was supposed to keep your dad company while you talk to your mum, remember?"

He waved to his mother in the bay window. "It's probably better this way. Mum looks upset. I'll need some moral support."

"Come on. Best get it over with, eh?"

Still clutching her handkerchief, his mother threw her arms around him and kissed his cheek. "I can't believe you're here, Colin. Why didn't you call?"

He glanced at Leanne. "We had to go to Norfolk. I didn't know if there'd be time for a visit. Here's something for your birthday. Sorry I missed it yesterday."

"Don't you worry, dear. Having you here is the best present I could have. How long are you staying? Oh, never mind. Go into the living room, and I'll boil the kettle. The hall's no place for gossiping."

While Leanne sat in an armchair admiring a Chinese patterned fire screen, Colin gazed at the tiny back garden through an open sash window. "It's hard to think I grew up here. I bet my first bike is still in that shed. Dad never throws anything away."

Cups clinked on saucers as Colin's mother stepped up from the kitchen. "I was only saying yesterday to your father how nice it'd be

to have you visit, and here you are. Made my day you have, dear."
She placed a tray on a small dining table pushed against one wall
and glanced at Leanne. "You've brought a young lady home, too."

Out of his mother's sight, Colin made a face. "Leanne's my boss,
and we share an apartment."

Colin's mother pulled out a chair. "It sounds complicated to me.
I'll never understand young people today. It right upset me when you
didn't come home for Christmas. Don't you care about your mother
anymore, Colin? I've not been well you know."

He was relieved when Leanne intervened. "Look, I'm not sure
what you think Mrs…"

"Call me Ellen, dear. No need to be formal."

A discreet nod from Colin told Leanne he was ready. "Well,
Ellen, your son is not only the best boatbuilder on my team, but he's
also my best friend. He has something important to tell you and
asked me to be with him. It might be upsetting for you both."

Colin sat by his mother at the table. "This isn't easy for me, and
the last thing in the world I want to do is hurt you, but I can't hold it
in any longer." He took a deep breath. "Do you remember when I
was little, you often said I should have been a girl?"

Ellen nervously stirred her tea. "That's a silly thing to say. I said
nothing of the sort."

He could see that she was embarrassed. "You did, mum … and I
never wanted toy cars or soldiers to play with."

"Your father made you a model of the boat he was on in the war.

You loved that. It's still in your room."

"Yeah, my fifth birthday, it was a fantastic gift. Do you remember what you gave me?"

His mother smiled. "Your Enid Blyton book of Fairies. It's in the bookcase in your bedroom."

"I kept it safe because it's just as precious to me as dad's boat. I love you, mum. But there's something you should know, and there's no easy way I can tell you … I've been living as a girl for nearly a year."

His mother looked bewildered. "I don't know what to say." She pulled a handkerchief from her sleeve and dabbed her eyes. "I've always tried to be a good mother. Where did I go wrong?"

"You did nothing wrong." He palmed his chest. "In here, I've always been your little girl. But it took Leanne to find her for you."

Leanne made to get up. "I think I should leave you two alone."

Ellen sighed and waved her to sit down. "Please stay Leanne. I've known for a long time that this might happen. When I was carrying him, I knew I was expecting a girl. His dad said it was wishful thinking, but now I know I was right. I've always been a strong woman, never one to let things get on top of me." She attempted a smile at Colin. "When the time is right, I'll tell your father, but don't expect him to be overjoyed."

He leaned over and hugged her. "It's me who was wrong. I should've told you how I felt years ago, but I was afraid you wouldn't understand." He kissed her cheek. "When you've told dad,

I'll come back as your not so little girl. We have a lot of catching up to do."

She caught hold of his hand. "That will make me very happy… but I don't know what to call you now."

He blinked away a tear. "Next time I see you, mum, I'll be your daughter, Colette."

*

On Monday morning, while Colin took a closer look at the hire boats, Leanne telephoned her solicitors in Guernsey, then returned to the dining room where Lisa Godwin was gathering up her paperwork. "Well that's a relief, they have a London office who will deal with the legal purchase and money transfer. I've asked them to make it a priority. We'd like to take over as soon as possible."

Lisa closed her briefcase. "I'm sure you'll both be happy here, Leanne. I was certain you'd want to occupy quickly, so this morning I called the vendor. He's agreed for you to move in before the contracts are signed, if you want to."

"Oh, that's very generous of him. I know Colette will be pleased. She's keen to start modernising the hire fleet."

Lisa grinned. "Richard tells me she's an exceptional boatbuilder, and a singer-songwriter, too. My daughter should be somewhere around. Claire insisted on coming with me today. She couldn't wait to meet the writer of one of her favourite songs."

Leanne walked with Lisa to her car. "By the way, the local garage is servicing the Transit van today. I've cancelled our return flights for tomorrow. We're driving down to Weymouth tonight for the early morning ferry. If all goes to plan, we'll be back next weekend."

Throwing her briefcase onto the back seat, Lisa grinned at muffled music coming from the studio. "It sounds like Claire has found Colette."

Leanne paused just inside the studio door. While Claire played rhythm guitar, Colette was holding a microphone. With eyes closed, she was singing, *You Don't Have To Say You Love Me*.

Lisa turned to Leanne. "I've never heard that song performed with such feeling."

Leanne nodded. "It's the reason we're leaving Guernsey. There's someone she needs to forget."

Chapter 18 - You said that once before

For months, Leanne had fought to keep the boatyard at St. Sampson's solvent. Now the struggle was finally over, she was both relieved and sorry. However much she appreciated Richard's offer to take over the yard at such short notice, it wasn't easy breaking the news to people who had been a part of her life for so long.

She looked up from her notes and studied each gloomy expression; Frank chewing something imaginary, as he so often did when presented with a problem. Bob taking longer than usual to roll a cigarette, and George leaning against the filing cabinet biting his lip. "So, I hope you'll all give Richard Seabourne the same support you've given me. He'll be taking over tomorrow and assures me that all your jobs are safe. It's not easy leaving you all, but I hope you'll understand that, for personal reasons, I have to move on." She handed two envelopes each to Bob and Frank. "As you know, Colette won't be coming back. She left work early on Friday without saying goodbye to you. She wanted to avoid an emotional scene. There's a personal letter from her in the white envelope; the brown one is a note and a thank you gift from me. Please don't open either of them until after I've left at lunchtime. That's it guys, I'll say a personal goodbye before I leave. George, please stay, I need to talk to you."

Looking glum, Frank and Bob shuffled out of the office. Leanne hoped for their sakes that Richard's plan to build sailing trimarans from scratch would be successful. She offered George a cigarette.

"Please sit down. How are things with Jeanette?"

"She's gone all mumsy. Having the baby has changed her. She's not the bitch she used to be. It's not what I wanted, but it's the way it has to be, isn't it?"

"Sometimes we have to make sacrifices for others. However much it hurts, all you can do is be the best husband and father you can." She handed him an envelope. "It's a bit more than I gave the lads, but this place would have gone under months ago if you hadn't joined the team. I've also put a small sum into a savings account for the baby. You can top it up, but only she can access it when she's eighteen. By then it will have grown into a useful sum. I hope that's alright." She handed him a folded document.

Opening it, he looked surprised. "This is very generous of you, Leanne. I don't know what to say."

"It's the least I can do, George. My kids never wanted for anything, except their mother. Their father saw to that." She swallowed back a rush of bile to her throat. She'd woken up this morning feeling queasy. Probably nerves at the prospect of painful good-byes. "James took every opportunity from soon after they were born to sideline me. To others, I was the mother who cared nothing for my children. I'll not make that mistake again." She paused, wondering why she'd opened up to George. "There's no letter from Colette, I believe she's already said goodbye to you."

"John brought a gift for the baby at the weekend. He told me Colette's gone back to being Colin. I've been trying to figure out why."

"Sorry, George. She asked me not to discuss her personal situation with you. She needs to make a new life for herself, and so do I."

George stubbed out his cigarette and fiddled with the envelope. "Well, thanks for this anyway. I'd best be getting back to work. I wouldn't want Richard Seabourne to think I've been idle."

Leanne raised her eyebrows. "You slacking? I doubt the thought would ever cross his mind. Richard didn't get to where he is today by chance, you know. He surrounds himself with bright, talented people, and he'll be looking for someone to replace Colette."

*

Apart from casual clothes that Colette would need for the journey to Norfolk, Colin packed everything he owned into the Transit van. Leanne would need help to load her things, but she wasn't due home until mid-afternoon. He needed to clear his mind, and the apartment wasn't the place to do that; it held too many memories.

From the viewing platform at Castle Cornet, Sark was just a smudge on the horizon. Away in the distance, a close-hauled sailboat reminded him of *Bethany*. The climb up to the Pilcher monument, George's hair falling forward at the picnic table, and his accepting kiss on the cliff path.

"What are you thinking, babe?"

"Jesus Christ, you startled me."

John leaned on the parapet. "You said that once before."

Colin smiled. "Yeah, on the lawn one Sunday afternoon a long time ago. You knew who I was all the time. How did you know I was here?"

"I saw you getting out of a minicab. By the time I'd parked the truck, you were looking at George's boat. I guessed it was your personal time, so I didn't disturb you."

"You called me babe, but I won't be Colette again until tomorrow when I leave the island."

John put an arm around Colin's shoulders. "You told me last week you were changing back, but you're still a babe to me. So, you're going back to the mainland as Colette … what gives?"

"Leanne's buying a boatyard in Norfolk. A fresh start for us both."

"Are you two an item now?"

"What else do I have, John?"

"You could have made it with George, he's still cut up."

"The baby needs him more than I do."

"George will never stop loving you."

"He told you that?"

"I know it, and Jeanette knows it too. I'll say no more." John turned away from the parapet. "Come here, you need a hug. I'll miss you. When you're settled, let me know where you are. And write more of those songs." He kissed Colin's cheek. "Your music will take off one day, you just gotta keep at it."

Colin turned away to gaze out to sea. "Yeah, I will. How's the album coming along?"

"Great! Well, it would be if we could find a record company willing to give us a chance. The boys are getting fed up with rejections. I guess our first single was a one-hit-wonder."

Richard Seabourne and his sister, Kay Ashton crossed Colin's mind. "Leanne has contacts, but first you need a professional recording studio."

John made a face. "You're joking, right? Have you any idea how much it costs to hire a studio to record an album? And anyway, they're all are booked up months ahead."

Colin gave John a sly look. "Apart from an all-girl band rehearsing in it, mine isn't being used."

"You've lost me, babe. You have a studio?"

"I couldn't believe it myself. The previous boatyard owner installed it. Give me a week or two to play with the equipment, then bring the boys over. It'll be fun to get together again, and you never know what it might lead to."

John stroked his beard. "And a girl band you say. Are they good?"

"Yeah, I think so. I jammed with Claire, the rhythm guitarist. She asked me to join them. But that's for the future. Right now, there's something you can do for me."

John feigned surprise. "Not here, babe. It's too public."

Colin grinned. "Daft sod! I just need a lift home."

The ride back to the apartment evoked memories of his time as

Colette; Creasey's department store opposite the harbour where George's boat was moored, and the Royal Hotel where she'd sung with the King Bees. Places that Colin wondered if he'd ever see again.

John pulled up just short of the courtyard. "You've got company, babe. Do you want me to come in with you?"

Colin had already spotted Jeanette sitting on the second step of the apartment stairs; little Colette's pram in the shade of the Transit van nearby. "No, I can handle it. I'll stay in touch." He waved John off and approached her. "Have you been here long?"

Jeanette stood up and straightened her skirt. "Just a few minutes. It's nice here anyway, quiet for the baby."

Colin peered into the pram. "Aww, she's as cute as ever." He turned towards Jeanette. "It's sweltering today. If you bring her up to the apartment, I'll make us a cold drink."

"Thanks, Colette. She'll probably wake up soon anyway. She's been restless in this heat."

Smiling at being called Colette, Colin collected the baby's bag from a wire basket under the pram then climbed the stairs. Wedging the door open, he put the bag in the living room and opened the French doors to create a cooling through draught. By the time he returned to the kitchen, Jeanette was in the hall holding her daughter. "Barley water alright?"

Jeanette nodded. "That'll be lovely. I expect you're wondering why we're here."

Colin took two tumblers from a shelf, opened a bottle of Robinsons, and retrieved a jug of iced water from the fridge. Whatever the reason for Jeanette's visit, it couldn't be any worse than the last time she'd arrived unannounced. "Not really, it's lovely to see the baby again." He ushered her through to the living room, motioned for her to sit down, and placed their drinks on the coffee table. "You do know I've gone back to being Colin, don't you?"

"It took me a long time to accept you as Colette, so I'd rather stick with that if you don't mind. Can you take the baby? I've got something for you."

Grinning, Colin cradled little Colette in his arms and stroked her cheek, and when she gripped his finger, his heart leapt. "Such beautiful blue eyes. I swear I can see George in her."

Jeanette rummaged in the baby's bag. "That's what his mum says. She came with us to the photographers last Saturday." She placed a large envelope on the coffee table. "We want you to have these. I'll take her now so you can look at them."

Colin withdrew two folded photo mounts. The first showed little Colette on a satin pillow, eyes open and grasping a tiny teddy bear. In the second, George standing beside his mother who looked as proud as any grandmother holding her first grandchild. "They're lovely, Jeanette. Thank you. But where are you?"

"I've got one here. I wasn't sure if you'd want it." Jeanette reached into the baby's bag again. "And Beth asked me to give you this. She said you'd understand."

Colin extracted a note from a small white envelope:

Dear Colette,

Please forgive me. When George told me what you'd done, I was angry. I wanted to give you a piece of my mind, but then I got to thinking. It takes a special woman to give up her own future for a father to be with his child. Whether you did the right thing or not, only time will tell. I know you'll come back to Guernsey one day, and my door is always open to you. Wherever you are and whatever you do, I hope you find the happiness that you deserve. Thank you for enabling me to enjoy my beautiful granddaughter.

All my love and best wishes. Beth. xx

Colin rushed into his bedroom. Beth meant well, but he didn't need this emotional turmoil. Plucking a tissue from a box on his dressing table, he wiped his eyes and returned to the living room. "Sorry about that, Jeanette. I'm a bit overwhelmed at the moment." He picked up an unframed photograph she'd put on the coffee table; with a wry smile, Jeanette was holding little Colette close to her face. "This one is lovely, I'd like to have it," he lied, fighting an urge to get the hell out of there before he broke down completely.

"I ought to be going. Baby doesn't seem to need her feed yet, and George will want his dinner when he gets home."

Colin picked up the baby's bag. "I'll take this down for you."

After making her daughter comfortable in the pram, Jeanette pulled up the sunshade and placed her bag in the wire basket. She turned to Colin frowning. "The whole world revolves around you, doesn't it, Colette? Everyone except me has to pretend to be nice to you."

Colin sighed. *What the fuck is she up to now?*

"You're too wrapped up in your misery to even consider that other people might have their own secrets. You don't know anything about me. You have no idea what I've been through."

"I'm not sure I want to hear this, Jeanette."

"You think I trapped George because I needed a man, any man. That's what Guernsey girls do, don't they?"

"Um, I think you should be going."

"Not until you've heard what I have to say." Jeanette took a step towards him. "At school, I had a best friend, we did everything together. We never gave a thought to boys."

Colin hoped she'd get this over with before it became too embarrassing. "I had a best friend, too." He thought of Samantha. "Most kids do at school."

"Did you want to spend the rest of your life with him?"

"Sam was a girl."

Jeanette nodded. "When we left school, Tammy trained to be a nurse. She had one of those bedsits near the hospital. I used to visit her often when she was off duty. It was fun gossiping about people we knew, pop music, all that girlie stuff. Then one day she went quiet and said there was something she had to tell me. She held my hands in hers and told me she loved me. She was deadly serious, but I didn't understand that at the time. Do you know what I did?"

259

"No, go on."

"I laughed at her. She told me she loved me, and I laughed at her, Colette. Can you imagine how she must have felt?"

Colin grimaced. "That's awful. What did she do?"

"She should have slapped my face and told me to get out. But Tam wasn't like that, she was the sweetest girl I've ever known. She kissed me and told me again that she loved me. I returned her kiss, and we spent the first of many happy times in her bed. In Tammy's arms I could forget about the abuse I was receiving at home. We pledged to spend our lives together after she qualified. Not a silly schoolgirl promise, but a real commitment. We even planned for me to get pregnant so we'd have a child. I loved that girl more than I could ever love any man."

"Do you still see Tammy?"

Jeanette's expression hardened. "Two years ago, on Christmas Eve, she was riding her bike home to St. Saviour; it had just started to snow. At Bailiff's Cross, a car lost control and ploughed into her. She died instantly. George was at the funeral, most of the island kids were. He helped me get over the grief, but he never knew that Tammy and I were lovers."

"Why are you telling me this, Jeanette?"

"Because you're the only person I know who could even begin to understand."

Colin shook his head. "I'm so sorry. I thought…"

"Yeah, you thought I was just a sad little girl with a whore for a mother. I know I was a bitch to you, Colette. I just didn't want to lose another person in my life." She hugged Colin and kissed his cheek. "I don't love George, but he's a good man, and he'll be a great father, and well ... there's all kinds of love, isn't there? One day he'll come looking for you. Until then I'll do my best to be a good wife and mother."

From beneath the elm tree, Colin watched Jeanette until she disappeared from view then returned to the apartment. After rinsing the tumblers, he was putting them back on the shelf when Leanne pulled into the courtyard. Her footsteps on the stairs sounded weary.

"Well that's over with, I can't say I'm sorry. I'll miss the lads at the yard though. How was your day, sweetheart?" She kissed his cheek.

"Coffee or a cold drink?"

"Cold please."

He took the tumblers back down from the shelf and reached for the Robinsons. "I saw John this morning. He's keen to bring the boys over to use the studio."

Kicking off her shoes, Leanne wiggled her toes. "Well, that's three then."

Colin took a deliberate close look at her feet, grinned, then poured the iced water. "Three?"

Leanne chuckled. "You idiot. Three acts! Kay Ashton said to start a new recording label, we'd need at least one good act. Now we've got three: You, Claire and friends, and The Shades."

261

"We're starting a record label?"

"Why not? What good is your studio without a way of marketing your product?"

"But we know nothing about the record business."

Leanne took a thoughtful sip of barley water. "You're right, we don't. But Richard Seabourne does, his sister is advising him."

"Oh, great! It's all worked out, and no-one bothered to ask me."

"Stop it, Colin! You're getting in a huff for no reason. Richard is coming over to Norfolk to see us next week. I stopped by his office on the way home. He's going to make us a very generous offer that we'd be silly to turn down. But you will have the last word, I promise."

He sighed. "I'm sorry. I'm still suffering from Jeanette's visit earlier. She brought some photos of the baby."

"Damn, I'd love to have seen her. Come on, we need to get my things in the van before we eat. I'll look at the photos later."

It took only an hour to fetch Leanne's belongings from the main house and load them into the Transit, even less from the apartment.

This would be their last meal before setting off for the ferry the following morning. It was too hot to cook, so while Leanne took the van to top up the tank, Colin prepared a salad. On her return, they sat down exhausted.

Spearing a last piece of tomato with her fork, Leanne glanced at the old bakelite radio. "That's our song, Colin. Remember?"

"I was about to say the same thing. *Go Now*, it's appropriate, isn't it?"

Leanne gave him a wicked look. "Our first real kiss."

Colin grinned. "Last August after your striptease. How could I forget?"

"It seems longer, sweetheart. I can't believe so much has happened in such a short time."

"Yeah, you're right. Before I came here, I tried to imagine what it'd be like. Don't laugh, but I even wrote a short story about all the things I thought I'd be doing."

"A short story? Bloody hell, with everything that's gone on, you could write a sodding book!"

He smiled. "Hmm, maybe I will one day, who knows."

She reached across the table for his hand. "Would you do it all over again if you had the chance?"

He squeezed her fingers. "I'd have no choice!"

She gave him one of her secret smiles. "And so would I, sweetheart."

Colin let go of her hand. "We're getting too sentimental. I'll fetch the photos."

Leanne opened the envelope. "Aww, she's beautiful, and that's the little teddy I bought her."

"I didn't know that."

"It was when I went out to buy the baby clothes. When I got back, you'd just dumped George. I didn't want to upset you further." She picked up the next photo. "Oh, George looks serious in this one, maybe it's because his hair is tied back. Beth looks very proud and grandmotherly, though."

Colin made a face. "Grandmotherly? I'm not sure that's a proper word, but it does suit her."

Picking up the last photo, Leanne grimaced. "This one's odd. Jeanette seems to be whispering something to the baby. It's not a good pose at all. Sometimes the photographer gives you the seconds unframed. Still, it's good of her to let you have it." She absentmindedly turned it over. "Did you notice she's written something on the back?"

"No. Is it something derogatory about me?"

"Listen, it doesn't make sense. *'I did it for you Tam, I'll never stop loving you.'* She's finally lost the sodding plot!"

He looked sheepish. His conversation with Jeanette earlier was personal, he couldn't reveal what Tammy meant to Jeanette. "Yeah, that's weird. I'll never understand that girl. Come on, let's get the washing up done. I want to go out this evening."

Leanne looked surprised. "Oh! We're travelling in the morning, I thought we'd have an early night."

"It's important to me, Leanne! I'll call a cab."

"Don't be silly, of course I'll take you. When do you want to go?"

He knew it would be emotional, but there was one last thing he needed to do before he left Guernsey. "I want to be at L'Erée before it gets dark."

Chapter 19 - A rose called Colette

With hardly a movement, the rising tide lapped the causeway, and a warm breeze caressed the coarse grass. Colin sat down. No blankets were needed tonight. Slowly, as the sun continued its nightly descent, the sky grew first pink, then orange. When it touched Lihou island, it seemed to grow. Its rising twin crept forward over shimmering seaweed strewn pools.

Giving up isn't easy. In fact, it hurts like hell.

Framed by colours that only an artist could replicate, Lihou finally became a silhouette. As the remaining edge of the fiery orb flared a last magical goodbye, he brushed a wisp of tear dampened hair from his eyes.

A hand gave his shoulder a comforting squeeze. He'd hoped for someone else but knew by her touch that it was Leanne. Looking up, he returned her secret smile. A tear on her cheek was tinted red in the fading light. Her blonde curls fell across his face. She kissed his lips, a soft sweet kiss that only a woman can give. Then she was gone.

A single lamp glowed on Lihou. He yearned for solitude, a time for his wounds to heal, a break from the suffering. But it wouldn't work, the misery was in his head. Loneliness would only make it worse.

Hugging his knees, he raised his eyes to the darkening sky above St. Mary's Priory. Would these same stars shine so brightly in Norfolk?

'If you want something badly enough, and reach out far enough, nothing is impossible.' He smiled, beautiful words to build dreams on, but nothing is real. Reaching up to pluck a star, a single rose fell into his hand.

George sat down. "Please don't be angry."

Colin sniffed the rose. "I'm not angry. I knew you'd come."

"That bloom is from your garden. I planted the bush next to where my shed will be to remind me of you."

"George Bisson, you're an old softie." He sniffed the rose again. "It smells sweet, what's the name of it?"

"It's called, Colette."

"It's a beautiful rose, thank you. Did you have to sneak out of the house?"

"I thought Jeanette would go off the rails when I told her where I was going, but she wanted to come with me. She's in the van with the baby. She told me she came to see you today."

"She did, I'll treasure the photographs."

George stared at the moonlit outline of Lihou. "Will you ever come back to Guernsey?"

Colin took a deep breath. "Maybe not for a long time, but I will be back."

"This is so bloody difficult for me, Col... Colin, I just need something to hold on to."

He put his arm around George's shoulders. "Hey, come on. Be strong. I didn't want it to be like this, pet."

"You called me, pet. You do still love me."

"I'm trying not to, but it's not easy."

George pounded the grass beside him. "It's not too late. Please come home."

"You know that's not possible."

"We could go somewhere else. Start over. Just you and me, like we said we'd do."

Colin remembered the plans they'd made and wished it were different. "For your sake and for little Colette, I have to move on. You must accept that."

George's hair fell forward. "Yeah, I know I do, but a part of my heart will go with you. Promise me you'll bring it back to me one day."

"If fate has that in store for us, I will. But before that can happen, I have to be complete in both my mind and my body. That will take time."

George stood up and held out his hands to him. "You've given me hope, I'll cling to it. Now it's my turn to ask for a kiss."

Careful not to crush the rose, Colin put his arms around George's waist. "Hold me tight, George. We can't make the world go away, but we can hide from it for a few moments."

Lifting Colin's chin, George spoke softly. "Colin or Colette, it makes no difference, I love you so very much."

Feeling George's lips touch his, Colin responded with passion; his tongue searching, tantalising. Deep down, he knew it wouldn't be the last time. Reluctantly, he pulled away. "It's time for you to go back to your daughter and her mother. Remember the promise we made under the elm tree. Until we're together again, we'll be joined in our thoughts every New Year's Eve."

"I won't forget, and I have another promise to make." He stroked Colin's cheek. "No matter how long it takes, I'll come here to watch the sunset one year from today, and the same day every year until I hold you in my arms again."

Savouring the sweet fragrance of a rose called Colette, Colin turned again to the silvery silhouette of Lihou. Behind him, he heard George drive away.

"Are you alright, sweetheart?"

Colin swung round. "I knew he'd come, Leanne."

"And I knew you knew he'd come."

He attempted a smile. "That doesn't make sense."

Leanne held his hand. "The baby is going to be beautiful."

"Yeah, little Colette will be a heartbreaker when she grows up."

"That's not what I meant, Colin. I need a hug, there's something you should know." Leanne's blonde curls caught the moonlight as she nestled onto Colin's shoulder. "Your birthday treat on Jersey was wonderful wasn't it?"

Even though Leanne couldn't see it, Colin smiled. "In the end, it turned out fine, didn't it? We should go to that hotel again, I know you enjoyed it."

Leanne looked up at him. "It worked wonders for you, too. You finally made love to me properly."

He closed his eyes and remembered the urgency, the pain when it happened, and the regret afterwards. "Yeah, the only time. I don't think I could do that again."

Leanne held his hand to her stomach. "You don't have to. Our baby is going to be beautiful."

Colin stared at her, his eyes glistening. "I can't believe it, Leanne. I'm going to be a father?"

Leanne thumbed a tear from his cheek. "No, sweetheart. Our baby will have all the love that two mothers can give. You don't have to say you love me, Colette. But I do love you."

Colette drew Leanne close and kissed her sweet lips. She closed her eyes, thought of George, and whispered, "I love you, too."

About the author

Born in Suffolk in the United Kingdom, Abigail Summer now lives in a small village in the north of France with her husband Alex.

As a teenager, she lived and worked in Guernsey. She made many wonderful friends with whom she shared the magic of the 1960s.

Years later, she returned and visited many of the places she'd known. Much had changed. The music scene in The Fermain Tavern was still vibrant though, and a band she was lucky enough to see played many of the old songs that she knew so well.

She couldn't leave without visiting one special place. The date was June 13th. She parked in the tiny car park at L'Erée and walked to the spot on the shore where, in this book, Colette said goodbye to George. After watching the spectacular sunset over Lihou, she sat on the coarse grass and wondered how different her life might have been had she not left the beautiful island that is Guernsey.

Dear reader,

Thank you for choosing my book. To receive prior notification of new novels and special offers, or just to say hello, please send an email to newsletter@abigailsummer.co.uk. I'm always happy to discuss my books with readers. If you've enjoyed Colette's story, you can help others to find my book by leaving a review on Amazon. Thanks in advance.

You can also interact with me on facebook.

www.facebook.com/SunsetOverLihou

LGBT in the 1960s

Today, we may think it odd that in the not too distant past, some aspects of being transgender could lead to a lengthy jail sentence. But in the 1960s this was all too true.

The word gay, adopted by people who prefer relationships with those of their own sex, was not widely used in the timeline of this book. Therefore, the author deliberately avoided using it.

The 1967 'Summer of Love' brought acceptance among young people of behaviours that were previously seen as taboo. Public demonstrations of same sex affection were rare. But in clubs, and at rock concerts, it wasn't uncommon to find two men or two women holding hands or kissing.

In July of 1967 homosexuality was decriminalised in England and Wales, the legal age of consent being set at 21. But in Guernsey, Gay men had to wait until 1983 for the same rights. It should be noted that same sex activity between consenting women has never been a criminal offence in Great Britain or Guernsey.

Although the author has written of Colette's acceptance as a woman by most of her friends, if prosecuted, Colin could have been convicted of gross indecency and sentenced to a term of incarceration or deportation. Thank goodness, as an enlightened society, we've legally abolished discrimination against vulnerable people like Colette.

Songs mentioned in this book

You Don't Have to Say You Love Me – Dusty Springfield

A Whiter Shade of Pale – Procol Harum

Go Now – The Moody Blues

Let's Spend the Night Together – The Rolling Stones

All I Really Want to Do – The Byrds

It Ain't Me Babe – Joan Baez

The House of the Rising Sun – The Animals

Hi-Heel Sneakers – Tommy Tucker

Dream – The Everly Brothers

Gonna Send You Back to Walker – The Animals

Dimples – The Animals

If I Fell – The Beatles

Yes it Is – The Beatles

Strange Brew – Cream

Then You Can Tell Me Goodbye – The Casinos

See See Rider – Ma Rainey

Prove It on Me Blues – Ma Rainey

Glamour Girl – (author)

Fool on the Hill – The Beatles

Moonlight Serenade – Glen Miller

I Only Want to be With You – Dusty Springfield

Printed in Great Britain
by Amazon

39920982R00166